To John

Caught in a
Cold War Trap

*Thanks for all [illegible]
[illegible] on the [illegible]
PD [illegible]*

Miller Caldwell

Best wishes

███ Clink
 ██ Street

London | New York

Published by Clink Street Publishing 2020

Copyright © 2020

First edition.

The author asserts the moral right under the Copyright, Designs and Patents Act 1988 to be identified as the author of this work.

ISBN: 978-1-913136-78-9 Paperback
978-1-913136-79-6 Ebook

In memory of Elizabeth Connie Caldwell,
who died far too young

About the Author

Miller Caldwell is a Scottish novelist. He graduated from London University having studied African industrial development, traditional African religions and the colonial history of West Africa. He has had articles published in health magazines and *The Scottish Review*.

In a life of humanitarian work in Ghana, Pakistan and Scotland, he has gained remarkable insights into human nature. He brought an African president to tears in West Africa in 2000 and he confronted Osama bin Laden in Abbottabad in 2006. He retired from being the regional reporter to the children's hearings in Dumfries & Galloway as he has mild cognitive impairment. He was, for twelve years, the local chair of the Scottish Association for The Study of Offending. He also served on the committee of the Society of Authors in Scotland as its events manager. This is his 23rd book.

Miller plays a variety of brass, woodwind and keyboard instruments. They cure writer's block. Married, he has two daughters and lives in Dumfries.

Contents

Chapter 1
Jura 1967

Have you ever been to the island of Jura? Not many people have. If you are a whisky connoisseur you possibly toured the island's distillery to taste the Isle of Jura single malt. Perhaps you were a climber assaulting the famous Paps of Jura, or a sailor assessing the treacherous cauldron of the Corryvreckan whirlpool from the safety of land. Maybe you needed to imbibe the presence of George Orwell (aka Eric Blair) who completed *Nineteen Eighty-Four* at Barnhill on the north of the island. That's about all you can do on Jura, which is why not many go there. That however, may be its attraction.

I was there during the Cold War and there my spying career took roots. I was on a family holiday in July 1967. In the third week, my life changed forever.

My name is Robert Harvie and on that holiday I turned sixteen years of age. My father was a Church of Scotland minister. Minister's families were not rich, so the holidays were the only real perks we enjoyed. Dad would bring four sermons with him each summer and the pulpit exchange was complete when our manse in Glasgow was occupied by the minister whose manse we lived in for a month. We usually enjoyed somewhere with fresh sea air, while the other minister and his family explored the culture of the Gallus Glaswegians, their numerous parks and the animated city which 'Smiles Better' with its keen sense of humour.

It was a wet morning. I remember that well. A real humdinger of a downpour, I heard my father say. I stood in the small north facing wooden porch while the salty air filled my lungs. The rain made the nearby coastline of Mull of Kintyre invisible. I cursed this four-week island break for being neither summer, nor a holiday. I longed to be home in the city engaging in the many different interests I had.

By lunchtime, the rain had retreated. A tiny patch of blue sky fought through the grey cloud, offering a ray of hope. The land in slow progress began to have a re-birth. Colours became vibrant once more and the single track road's tarmac glistened. I focussed on a snail crossing the road. It was not risking a car's approach; few cars were on the island but I feared a seagull might be tempted to devour the slow-moving creature. I ran towards it in haste. I picked up the snail and placed it on the grass verge. It felt good—a good deed accomplished on a boring day. The snail was insecure and unwilling to reappear from its shell at first. I waited in silence. It did too. Then I smiled as it continued its journey into grassy cover.

I turned around and saw the sun settle on a verdant hillock behind the manse. I decided to get to its summit and take the family Bush radio with me. My mother approved my plan and I set off. It was a steep climb and my route was circuitous—to avoid calf strain. I stopped and turned around. I saw a tanker in the distance. It moved slowly like that reluctant snail I helped cross the road. I imagined myself on the ship, going somewhere exotic. It was sailing down the Firth of Clyde after all, and that perhaps meant an American trip, even South

America. There again it might just be going to Ireland. My thoughts came back to land.

The swirling wind dictated which way my blond hair would flow as I arrived breathless on the crest of the hill. My foot caught a heather clad mound. Then I saw I had caused a disturbance to the zigzag of an angry adder. It moved like a retracting hose away from me and I relaxed. I forgot to mention—Jura had a number of vipers lurking in the undergrowth in the hills. On warm sunny days, they could be seen on any open land squirming around on the warm ground. I found a flat grassy bank and sat down.

The Bush radio gave me the Home Service and the Light programme. I could not concentrate on their urban offerings so changed the button at the top to short wave and turned the dial. I caught some French programme and lingered to hear an excited high-pitched Parisian woman. It could advance my French studies, which would resume in two weeks' time back at school. However, after I had heard a sentence or two of her rapid French fire I could not follow her line of thought. I turned the dial further on. This time I heard a farming report. I gave up re-tuning. I kept the station on and lay back to absorb some sun. I could have fallen asleep in a matter of moments but there was something odd about the programme.

The announcer spoke about English Ayrshire cows. What a howler. That was akin to saying Eccles cakes come from Aberdeen. There was more to confuse me. The reporter spoke about the 12 coal mines in Suffolk, the powerhouse of energy for the south of England. Suffolk coal? I knew these facts to be wrong and waited for the punch line. It never came. When the programme ended the announcer informed me that *Farming Matters* would broadcast at the same time next week, on Radio Moscow.

It was not a comedy after all, but an inaccurate description of British farming and land use. I felt indignation; an urge to respond, to clear up their misinformation. After all, I had little else to occupy my time. So that night in bed I wrote a letter explaining that Ayrshire cows were from Ayrshire, in Scotland, and Suffolk was farming land and did not have a coal seam—as I recalled from my school geography notes.

The following day I took my letter, addressed to Radio Moscow, Moscow, U.S.S.R. to the Craighouse post office, which was in a cottage. A red post box outside gave the clue that the postmistress lived inside. I entered setting off a bell clanger above my head. A woman came through from her lounge, closed the door behind her and sat down on a floor screeching wooden chair by her ink padded desk. She read the address.

'Moscow? That's foreign,' she confirmed in a matter-of-fact voice and opened a book. Two fingers ran down the columns like sprinters. 'Anything in the letter I should know about?' she asked.

I hesitated. My heart seemed to stop beating for a moment. I supposed I could share its contents with her. 'I have written to them to show there were mistakes in one of their programmes.'

She looked at me through horn-rimmed glasses. 'I don't need to know what you write. So, is it just paper inside?'

I nodded somewhat embarrassed. She took her fingers from the list then snapped the book closed.

'Then that's nine pence postage. It might take a few days to get there.'

Phew, I expected to pay more. She returned the letter to me and I took it to the post box outside. As it dropped down into dark oblivion I wondered how soon she would retrieve it and have it sent seaward, landward and forward to Moscow.

Chapter 2
Glasgow 1970 – 1974

After I got home from that miserable wet holiday with too many raw seaweed memories of Jura still lurking in my mind, a letter arrived. It was from London. It bore the embossed markings of the Russian Embassy on the back flap. I kept it hidden from my parents.

As anticipated, the station appreciated my contact and was delighted to acknowledge the corrections to their farming programme, which I had supplied. To show their gratitude, I would receive a package in the near future. And I did, about three weeks later. Inside a brown packet were three photographs. One was of the Kremlin and two of Red Star Square both at night and in the day. In addition were Radio Moscow UK listening times in a handy booklet, a personal letter and an ornament of the famous Red Square in a glass hemisphere, on which snow fell every time it was shaken. The letter was from Olga Lagonov. She wished to be my pen friend.

Olga and I exchanged letters monthly for three years and my interest in the Russian language grew. We corresponded about football—her brother was a Spartak Moscow supporter like her. We rarely wrote about politics; more the things that interest teenagers. However, any romance was out of the question for obvious geographical and cultural reasons, although she was a very attractive girl, as her photo which I kept in my wallet showed.

The relationship lasted this length of time because Olga was by now my Russian tutor. I had studied Russian in my final year at school, but with her support, it led to me gaining excellent results in the language. Of course, nobody knew about Olga. I even kept her correspondence from my parents, sometimes with difficulty. I became somewhat furtive in gathering the mail. When they eventually learned of my pen-friend in Russia they decided it an impossible relationship which would wither in time. Fortunately, their suspicions were not raised any higher.

The Russian language was on offer as a subsidiary subject, after French and Spanish, on the modern languages degree course at Glasgow University. I enrolled. Neither did this fact worry my parents. They felt that eventually after the cessation of the Cold War, the rapprochement was necessary and that knowing the Russian language would be a good way to join the Foreign Office, perhaps. I did not dissuade them.

Before the start of my first term at Glasgow University, I received a letter from London. It was from the Russian Ambassador's office once more. Inside was a cheque to cover my living expenses for the first year.

I looked at the cheque. £2,000.

I had never held such an amount of money in my hands before. It would more than cover all my accommodation, books, meals, and I guessed several beers. Yet I had also been given, by the British government, the maximum student grant, as my father's stipend was deemed insufficient to support me.

I focussed on the passage in the letter where it stated 'for the first year'. Did that mean similar amounts would arrive in time for each of my four years? What if I sent the cheque back to the embassy? Would they be offended?

I held on to the cheque for four days before deciding to bank it. During that time I wondered why they were so generous. Surely my original letter was forgotten by now? It could hardly be a bribe to engage in work for them as I was now engaged in a lengthy study. In the end, I put it down to good fortune; to a moment of serendipity. After all, I had been corresponding with Olga for some considerable time and had not been compromised in any way.

When I told her I was studying Russian as well on the modern languages course, Olga was delighted and ensured I was fluent in Russian and could write in their Cyrillic script with ease. This pleased my lecturers.

My new Glasgow address, a small flat in Gardner Street in the west end, was ideal in many ways. It was quite near the university and gave me the privacy my mail required. I arranged for it to be re-directed from home of course. Olga too was at university. She was already in her second year at the Lomonosov Moscow State University studying biochemistry.

Over the next four years her letters arrived sporadically and mine were sent at a similar rate. Their infrequency upset me at first. After all, she had given me a good grounding in their language, and I hoped to continue to write in Russian to her.

Meanwhile, without fail, the London embassy sent me radio listings. I did tune into Radio Moscow from time to time, naturally. Balalaika music was a change from Scottish country dancing tunes, but I'd give the wrong impression if you thought I returned from lectures and spent each night in the flat. I had a social life. I played rugby for the university and I joined the music society. I also attend meetings of the Russian club.

The club's membership included a collection of leftist Marxist students in love with the 1917 revolution and sympathetic to the land and people who suffered so much, as allies, in World War Two. They knew Conservative governments were traditionally hostile to Russian communism, so the change from Labour's Harold Wilson to high Tory Edward Heath strengthened the club's membership. There was talk of a visit to Russia. As well as Moscow, Leningrad was high on their agenda, but finances held them back. I wondered if my wealth could be put to the common good, but having what was then a considerable amount of money was likely to alienate me in their communist eyes.

Then I found a girlfriend. Or perhaps she found me. It was a very sudden, mutual and powerful attraction. She was not from the Russian club. I met her at a music society weekly meeting.

Morag Sutherland was a Lanarkshire girl from Motherwell. Lean and sporty, she had a smile which melted my heart. Medicine was her subject and I knew she'd still be studying after I graduated, which might end our blossoming relationship. But what the heck? I had to start romancing sometime, somewhere.

We drank coffee during the day and at the weekends, in the evenings, she sipped gin in the pubs we visited while I drank beer, or more often cider. We spoke about our upbringings and found a few names of contempories we knew in common. She told me she was glad to meet someone who was not a medic. All her fellow students were, of course, but so too was her father, mother, brother and sister. No wonder she was pleased to encounter me, I thought. It wasn't long before we held hands in public. It felt good to announce we had each other.

We visited each other's flats. I stroked my hands through her lush black tresses, and it wasn't long before more intimate strokes satisfied us both. It took us to another level and a commitment to one another, as many student affairs did likewise. After all, she was my first girlfriend, and I was her first boyfriend. It was new territory for us both and we were glad to progress our discoveries in harmony.

I wrote to Olga informing her of my new acquaintance. I wondered how she would react, as our letters had the intimacy of a brother/sister relationship. I need not have worried. She congratulated me and told me she had a boyfriend. She had had him for more than a year. That saddened me. She had never told me about him. What else could she be keeping from me?

After four years of study, graduation called for a family gathering. My parents attended the Bute Hall, where the ceremony took place and they met Morag for possibly the fourth or fifth time. Photos were taken of me in a black gown with a purple hood signifying that I was now a graduate Master of Arts. I clasped the rolled certificate in my hands. Then my father offloaded the qualification while my mother took photos of me and some with Morag clinging on to my arm. This ritual was replicated all over the university lawns and a bright sunny day in June was appreciated by all—a relief for so many Glaswegians.

The following morning I began to think about what I would do with my qualification. I contemplated teaching languages in a secondary school. That meant a year of further study, of course. I had better get my application in. But which college of education should I approach? One in Glasgow, Morag hoped, as I did too.

Then on Saturday morning, as I left the kitchen, I saw an envelope fly through the letterbox and land like a plane as it taxied to a stop on the varnished wooden hall floor. It was a letter from the Russian Embassy containing a card congratulating me on my degree.

In the accompanying pages I learned I was invited to the Russian Embassy, an invitation which came with a rail ticket. I could hardly refuse to attend—the golden goose had, after all, seen me comfortably through my student days. It seemed appropriate that I should go to show my appreciation.

Chapter 3
A visit to The Russian Embassy

When I told Morag I had an invitation to visit London she was curious. I suppose she feared I might get a job there and the distance would put our relationship under strain.

I came clean.

'The Russian Embassy?' she said raising her voice.

'Yes, well you know I studied Russian, I speak and write the language?' I said as if butter would not melt in my mouth. It was information she knew anyway.

'Yes, but…' she stuttered.

'Yes, I know. London seems far away, but there's nothing definite. I can't imagine they are going to offer me a job down there. After all, if it was a job offer, the letter would have said so. Wouldn't it?'

She nodded slowly, glum-faced. I came close and wrapped my arms around her shoulders. 'Perhaps I should have studied medicine,' I whispered into her ear.

She turned her face and kissed my cheek. 'God no, we need someone who isn't a doctor in the family.'

Her words should have appeased me. Instead, there was a hint in how she said about 'in the family' which made me feel uneasy. She had arrived at that point before me. In truth, I was very much unsure of what lay ahead for me, or if it would be with Morag. I hoped my confused feelings did not show.

The early train journey down south was uneventful. I passed the time trying to identify what different passengers did. Business diaries seemed ubiquitous but gave nothing away. Their newspaper choice did.

I had lunch in the dining coach. As the waiter, in a white jacket, approached with the terrine of soup I noticed I was the youngest diner by far. He lodged his foot against the table leg with his thigh resting on the table as he served his ladle into my soup plate. My finances allowed for this luxury and I suppose it made me feel important.

Shortly after 2 p.m. the train arrived at Euston station. I took the district line to Bayswater and proceeded along the road of the same name. There bearing down on me was the red background of a flag, with the gold hammer and sickle beneath a gold star—the flag of the Soviet Union.

I entered through the iron gates and saw the light coffee coloured stone building. I climbed twelve steps and entered the embassy. I approached the reception desk with a smiling blond woman eyeing my approach.

'Good afternoon, can I help you?' she asked in her guttural Muscovite voice. After I greeted her in Russian I told her I had a letter and took it from my jacket. I handed it to her. She seemed to speed read its contents.

'A moment please,' she said lifting the telephone. 'Василий Чазов.'

I heard her ask for Vasily Chazov, the author of my letter. I looked forward to meeting him. She replaced the receiver and turned towards me. 'Mr Chazov will be ready for you in a moment.'

Pictures of Leonid Brezhnev adorned the wall opposite me. He had been the president since my original Jura letter to Radio Moscow, all those years ago. I did not have to wait long.

'Come this way please,' she ordered and I followed like

a collie dog. We walked along a corridor filled with framed photographs of other Soviet leaders before abruptly stopping as we turned the corner. She knocked on the dark wooden door. She waited a moment with her ear to the door then entered.

'Mr Harvie, come,' she said with an arm welcoming me.

Vasily Chazov was a ruddy-faced cherub of a man—almost too large for his light grey suit. He was strong and of good height, with the apparent charm of a ladies' man.

'Delighted to meet you, at last, Mr Harvie,' he said rising from his seat and offering his hand.

I shook it firmly. 'More so I,' I replied. 'You secured my financial affairs when I was at university. That was very much appreciated.'

'Ah yes,' he said smiling at me. 'Many congratulations on your degree. It is a significant milestone, Robert.'

I smiled at him as I sat down. First name terms already. A bit premature for me to follow suit, I decided.

'Modern languages. Great skill and much in demand these days,' he continued.

'I was wondering whether I could be a school teacher, sharing my language skills with the next generation.'

He nodded, stroking his chin. 'An admirable thought,' he said and then his face took on a more quizzical look. 'I thought a young man like you might want to see a bit of the world first.'

'Naturally, but I haven't thought about that. I have a girl-friend back in Scotland to consider.'

'Ah yes, Morag. Still a few years to go for her before she qualifies, not so?'

I hesitated for a moment. 'Yes, a few years to go yet,' I said knowing he saw me thinking how he knew about Morag. He smiled and opened a box of cigarettes. He offered me one. I shook my head. He lit his cigarette and sat back in his chair. He had two cushions behind him. The smoke rose to the ceiling.

'You wonder how I know about Morag?' he asked with a slight smirk of a smile.

I nodded, not finding the words to indicate my surprise, my intrigue and my interest.

'Olga told me. She is my niece.'

'Oh, I see,' I said not really understanding how or why Olga's letters had come his way. Nor why Olga had never told me about her uncle. But soon the conversation changed.

'I suppose you are still wondering why I thought we should meet?'

Once more I nodded, but my senses were sharp and I paid even greater attention this time.

'I'd like to offer you a job.'

'A job? Really?'

'Yes, a job in West Africa, Ghana to be precise.'

Did I hear right? My eyes narrowed in disbelief. 'Africa! My goodness. But...but what would I do there?'

'Let me make it clear, this job had been cleared by Leonid Brezhnev, the President himself.'

His eyes pierced mine. He wanted to see my response. But he did not wish to hear me yet. He gave me a history lesson.

'You remember October 1962? The American's attempted to overthrow Fidel Castro at the Bay of Pigs? It was a disaster. So Castro asked us to help out as the so-called Cuban Missile crises ensued.'

'Yes I was 11 at the time. It was a frightening time,' I recalled. For almost a fortnight it felt the end of the world might come about as the giant political powers stood up to each other.

'President Kennedy and Comrade Khrushchev played games. But Russia was far from Cuba. We needed a half-way refuelling base to aid Castro. Guess where we found it?'

A picture of the world rotated in my mind and then I saw a possibility. 'Was it Ghana?' I asked

'Right the first time, but not in its capital, Accra. We got permission to use the large airport at Tamale in the north of the country—the dry undeveloped north. It became a Russian base for our aircraft to refuel on their way to Cuba. Kwame Nkrumah was keen to get Russian aid and we gave him some agricultural machinery into the bargain. The British never supported him, so he became our friend.

'Today, the airport is underused. It is mainly a domestic route, only a few planes land in a week. The locals are poor; they travel by road—no matter how dangerous that can be. Many travel south to eke out a living.'

'I still don't see how I could work there,' I said hoping I looked sufficiently interested and vacant at the same time.

'We need to open the airport up, for our use. Make our presence felt. The north of Ghana has one crop that never fails. Monkey nuts. You know groundnuts or you call them, peanuts—not so? They grow by the wayside as well as in scrub lands. They can produce groundnut oil, it has great potential.'

'When you say 'potential,' in which market and how much groundnut production is there?'

He smiled at me. 'Good questions. The health benefits of peanut oil include: better skincare, lower cholesterol levels, improved heart rates and a stronger nervous system. It also boosts cognitive function, strengthens the immune system, and lowers blood pressure. Need I say more?'

'Wow, that's amazing. But why don't the Ghanaian people export it themselves?'

He smirked. 'They just roast the nuts and eat them. None of them sees the potential. We provided the technology and production know-how. That's where you come in. You, Robert, will be the manager of the Tamale Pioneer Groundnut Export Company.'

I guffawed. 'But I know nothing about business, no idea how to get the groundnuts and have no financial or administrative skills.' Sweat was beginning to congregate on my brow.

'I said you would be the manager. Not the General Manager. Igor Utechin is there already, he will show you the ropes. He is expecting you. His English is at times limited. He is from Yekaterinburg. He needs an English speaker and someone who speaks Russian. Are you interested?'

My mind could not work fast enough. 'I think I can't answer yet. I'd need to talk to Morag.'

His smile did not disappear. It grew larger. 'She could do her elective weeks at the Korle Bu Teaching hospital in Accra. We could fly you down each weekend. Now that would help out, not so?'

'Well maybe. But what if I turn down this very kind opportunity?' I asked with a lump of fear in my throat.

His smile disappeared. 'Come, come Robert. We did not fund your education for nothing. It's time to pay back some, isn't it?' he said, his manner both threatening and paternal. 'Our conditions are good. You'll have an annual leave of one month. We fly you back home after three years. A salary in cedis, the local currency, and £150 a month put into your account in Scotland.' His smile seemed sincere, yet his poise unsettled me.

In fact, I felt trapped. I could not see a way out. I had landed myself a job, for which I was thankful, but his tone had changed and for the first time those student cheques came with conditions.

He rose from his seat and went to a locked cabinet. He opened it. Two glasses appeared and then a bottle of vodka. He poured and offered me a drink. The glass was cut crystal. He stood in front of me and clicked my glass. 'To your decision, by tomorrow.'

'By tomorrow?' I said. 'Then I must be on my way to find a place to stay overnight.'

He shook his head. 'We have a hotel for you. Send the bill to me.'

I gulped the rest of the vodka down and returned the glass to his desk. I ought to be grateful, but I wondered if I was destined for darker things.

My stay was at the London Chesterfield hotel in Mayfair. After a sumptuous steak meal served with panache. I had an ice cream coated by warm chocolate sauce served over exotic fruit and then a coffee. Throughout this dinner, I tried hard to find the words I needed. Then I returned to my room, sat on the seersucker blue bedspread and telephoned Morag.

'Hi darling, Robert here.'

'Hi pet, where?'

'The Chesterfield hotel in Mayfair.'

'Mayfair wow. Why?'

'Well, I was offered a job.'

'In London?' she fired back with smoking gun rapidity.

'London? No...' I said twirling the telephone cord around my fingers

'That's a relief. So where, Glasgow?' she suggested with a charming lilt in her voice. The line went silent for a moment. The time had come to break the hard news.

'I've been offered the appointment of manager at the Pioneer Groundnut factory in Tamale, northern Ghana.'

'What?' she almost screamed. 'You are joking surely,' she said in a very slow tortured voice. 'You've no idea what a manager does and in Africa. Good god.'

'I know but I'll be shown the ropes. There is a man in overall charge.' I sensed a frown was appearing on her forehead. 'And the good news is that you can come out to the teaching hospital in Accra during your elective period.

Korle Bu Teaching Hospital, it's called. That would be good.'

'Hang on. Groundnut factory in Ghana? I just can't believe this. Er...so how long would you be in Africa for?'

'There's one month's home leave.'

I untwisted the telephone cord, stood up and gazed unfocussed out of the window.

'So, if you take this job that means years without you?'

'I'll write regularly,' I pleaded. But the line went dead. I knew she was upset and I ended the call. It would be a long night.

Chapter 4
Making a Break

I was back in the Embassy by half past nine the following morning. I must have crossed at least four roads on my way over but I could not remember doing so. My morning walk was accompanied by the sounds of busy traffic but it was muffled. I was engrossed in what I might face that morning.

Comrade Chazov was in a serious mood. He sat crunched up in his swivel chair. He spoke in Russian, of course. He told me a passport for Ghana had been ordered for me. Instinctively, I told him my passport was in Glasgow. He leered at me.

'Your Russian passport—and you will have diplomatic status, so no need for a British visa.'

That made me a Russian subject. How easily I had slipped into that role, one which was deeply uncomfortable. God, what the hell was happening to me?

'So, Africa. Are you set to go?' Comrade Chazov asked, and he sat back to hear my answer. I was slow to reply.

A multitude of questions filled my mind. Yes, what an experience Africa would be and Ghana was a Commonwealth country. I'd be welcomed but as a Russian citizen? Just what was I doing?

'I... I... I just can't believe how quickly this is happening.

Does this mean I'm no longer British? I asked in a strained voice. 'How can I explain that to Morag? How will my parents react?' Comrade Chazov saw the anxiety in my face.

'Relax, Robert. You will still be Scottish, I mean British. But to get you into Ghana and working with a Russian in Tamale, it makes sense to have a Russian passport, not so?'

I relaxed. I saw the sense in what he said. However, that was just one matter dealt with.

'Preparation will take a bit of time. You will need yellow fever injections and some anti-malarial pills too, but we will arrange that.'

'So will I have time to go back to Scotland?'

'Yes, you can go tomorrow, for a week if you like. Let your family know you have accepted a job to produce groundnut oil. No other details are required.'

'Then I can get a train back tonight,' I said feeling I needed time to come to terms with this development.

'No tomorrow morning. One of our embassy doctors will see you this afternoon and give you your yellow fever injection and some Malarone. You will have to start that course immediately to build up your immunity against malaria,' said the avuncular Russian

'Malaria?'

'Yes, you don't want to catch that, do you?'

I recalled West Africa is known as the white man's grave. God, I hoped I would survive and not be that White Man.

'So, how long will I be there?'

Comrade Chazov sucked an invisible sweet as he contemplated his answer. 'It may be two, could be a three -year tour, with a break in the middle. That's common for the white people in West Africa.'

I thought how the last two years of university had flown by. Anyway, it wasn't a prison sentence; in my mind, it was becoming an opportunity.

'So tomorrow morning, Glasgow?'

'Yes of course, but you must return by next Thursday night. Your flight to Accra is on Friday morning.'

'From Heathrow?' I asked.

'Yes Robert, Heathrow,' he replied. He thought for a moment before asking, 'One thing I should have asked. Do you have any allergies?'

I didn't need to think about that. 'Chocolate, anything with chocolate—it brings me out in hives, horrible hives,' I said recalling the last time I ate some chocolate, which had been eight years ago. 'I can't even take chocolate cake,' I added for good measure.

'Interesting, chocolate,' he said writing as he spoke.

Stations flew by in a blur as the train progressed north. Towns and fields had a regular sequence to follow but my mind lost interest in their sameness, that morning.

Had I not accepted the money in my first year at university I'd be facing a class hoping to learn some French or Spanish. Only senior classes might wish to learn Russian. But I had slipped into an unknown world. Well, unknown except I'd be in Africa in a week in a job for which I had no training or experience— and I knew the separation would strain my relationship with Morag. It was to her I had to make my first visit.

I knocked on the door of her flat. From inside I heard the call of 'coming.' My heart thumped like a marauding elephant— my mind was already in Africa. Then the door opened.

'Robert, darling. What a surprise.'

I hugged Morag with a strength which surprised me. Could this be our last embrace?

'Yes, took the train this morning. I didn't want to disturb your classes.'

21

She kissed my cheek then separated abruptly.

'Let me make you a coffee—I need to know more about these plans you have,' she said.

She took two mugs from the kitchen cupboard and spooned in some granules of instant coffee. I noticed her mug had a half-risen sun with the text New Horizons. Mine simply stated Coffee Mug. As I poured in a splash of milk, the inquiry began.

'So, Robert, this job is not just about you, is it? It's about us.'

I nodded as I sat down on the sofa. Morag did not sit beside me. She sat opposite to concentrate on interrogating me about my plans.

'Did you really want this job, or was your hand forced?'

I smiled and nodded at the same time. Morag was perceptive.

'A manse son, with apparently no shortage of money. Didn't that seem odd to you?' I asked.

'Now that you say it…'

'I've led a double life for almost six years now.' Then I launched into my downfall, starting with the trigger on that lonely island, Jura. Morag listened as if assessing the demeanour of a mental health patient contemplating suicide.

When I took breath, after some fifteen minutes, she said, 'It's going to be hard, very hard for us.'

My nod was minimal. 'I'm at a loss what to say other than, Morag, you are my true love and I'd not sacrifice that for anything.'

She approached me and took my hands in hers.

'We'll see. You keep your promise and I'll keep mine.'

I felt what she said set the ground rules fairly. I pulled her towards me. Our cheeks lay against each other's and our bodies began to quiver. The tears then trickled down our faces.

My parents were thrilled to learn I was going to the former Gold Coast. They recalled the missionaries who had served there since the Basel and Bremen missions welcomed the Church of Scotland in 1914. Their combined efforts had established not only many primary and secondary schools but hospitals and churches too. My father even found in his church yearbook the names of the current ecclesiastical staff abroad. He said I should get in touch with Rev. Willy Salmond of Ridge Church in Accra. I took note of his name along with some others he suggested. I kept the Russian connection from my father and mother. I had started to lie with consummate ease. That concerned me.

I spent the next few days buying tropical attire. Nothing too garish of course; just a half dozen short-sleeved shirts and a couple of pairs of light trousers. And a sturdy pair of shoes would not come amiss if I faced a surprised reptile.

My daily course of anti-malarial tablets were already underway. They were small and white and packed a nasty taste. With only a couple of days left in Glasgow, I suggested an evening meal.

The Ubiquitous Chip was handy, halfway between the university and Morag's flat. There at a table for two we sat looking into each other's eyes. Morag seemed close to tears as we waited for our orders.

'I can't help but feel you are about to become a Russian spy.'

The thought was never far from my mind. Yet I had dismissed it until now. 'No, this is nothing to do with spying. It's about peanuts. They need someone who can speak both Russian and English to help a Russian General Manager of a groundnut oil company—he's struggling with the language, they tell me. I can see their need. No, it can't be a spying role.'

I could almost hear her brains ticking over.

'So you are off on Friday? From Heathrow, I presume?'

'Yes, that's right. If you had known my first job was to be in Africa, perhaps we would not have had our first date?' I said.

She frowned. Her response was reassuring. She clasped my hands together, over hers.

'Don't talk like that, Robert. A girl's first love is important,' she told me.

My genuine smile acknowledged the fact. 'That's true for a boy too,' I replied.

'I bet there were some girls in your father's congregation who had an eye for the minister's son.'

I smiled as I recalled Lizzie and Pamela whose company I had enjoyed in Sunday school and Bible class and told Morag. But they had long ago faded into the distance. I had taken Morag to a deeper relationship, and that was why this meal was so difficult.

'Morag, you will soon be qualified. Your last placement can be in Ghana. Surely that would suit us? Tropical medicine, quite a feather in your cap.'

I was clinging to straws, but I liked the smile which my suggestion raised. My fork lurked over my plate. It eventually speared a sprout.

'It boils down to how much we love each other—doesn't it?' she said.

I chewed the sprout then forked some chips. 'Morag, I have no intention of finding love anywhere else. If you get to Accra for six weeks, then we will be less than a year apart. And I'll have some leave to take too. Time should fly by. Why would I have made that suggestion if I had decided to end our relationship?'

She tapped my hand. 'Then you still love me?'

My smile was broad. 'I love no one else. Yes, of course, I love just you, only you.'

'That's what I wanted to hear,' she said with her white teeth in full glow.

I was aware of the waiter approaching. He asked if the meal was enjoyable and we agreed it was. But he did not go away. He took the white wine from its cooler and topped up our glasses before he left us in peace.

'I love you, Robert. Of course, I do. I just know I will miss you.'

'I'll write to you every week.'

'Is that a promise?'

'It's my intention. I don't know what the job will be like. But I'll write as regularly as I can. Contact by letter will help you concentrate more on your studies, you know—with an absent boyfriend.'

Morag gave her dimple crater smile. I loved that expression of hers.

That last night before returning to London, I spent in Morag's flat. We sat on the couch watching the evening news with our arms around each other. Then she switched off the box. She approached me with a mischievous grin. She coaxed me with her index finger to her bedroom and we slept that night knowing it would be our last embrace for some time, or forever.

Chapter 5
Setting Foot in Africa

As the Terracotta Army of Qin Shi Huang was being unearthed at Xi'an, China, I stepped off the plane at Accra in overpowering humidity.

It was as if I had walked into a baker's oven. I was soon glad to find myself in the air-conditioned terminal to await my internal flight to Tamale. Itinerant sellers strolled by with offerings of sour kenkey dough, fried plantain and fresh oranges, many still in their green skins. I bought one.

It was as I peeled the orange that a young American man came to sit beside me.

'First time in Ghana?' he asked with no reserve.

'Yes, it probably shows,' I said before I offered the back of my sticky hand.

'Hi, I'm Bob Adams. American Peace Corps. A bit like your Voluntary Services Overseas, right? You British?'

God, what was I? Russian? Scottish? British? 'From Glasgow, Scotland,' I replied. 'But not with VSO. I'm going to manage a peanut factory in the north,' I informed him with a degree of pride. 'And you?'

He pointed to a satchel sitting between his feet. 'I teach at Navrongo Secondary School on the border with Upper Volta. Math is my subject. Well, in fact, math and music, the 'm' subjects.' Then he surprised me by saying, 'You going to Tamale?'

I squinted.

'Yes, how did you know that?'

'The big factories are in Tamale. It's the largest town in the upper region.'

Soon we were called to gate number 3 for Tamale. The Ghana Airways plane shone in the hot sunshine of the day and we felt the oppressive humidity once more as we boarded.

'Let's sit over there,' Bob said, and I knew I'd get no respite from his enquiries. I had no option but to agree.

There was no delay in getting off the ground.

'Just under an hour, this flight, but what a difference. You get sweaty in the south and as dry as a pretzel in the north. Gotta drink a lot.'

'Perhaps dry heat is the better option? Is fresh water freely available?'

He gave a paternal smile. He knew the ropes. I didn't.

'The market in town has bottled water. It's best to drink that. Anything else and you might get the galloping guts.'

'Hmm—not worth thinking about that,' I said.

'This is the white man's grave you know?' he laughed. 'Not really true,' he continued. 'It was the amount of gin the Colonials took with their quinine that gave rise to the name. Cirrhosis of the liver killed many of them, not only the female mosquito.'

I absorbed his insights, wondering if they might be outdated. 'Don't you think the colonial times are well behind us now, I mean, progress is being made all the time?'

He seemed to nod in agreement. 'Just don't forget one thing. When you are defeated in achieving something, as you sure will in Ghana from time to time, just recognise one word.'

My eyebrows raised in curiosity. 'And that word is?' I eagerly asked.

'WAWA,' he said laughing, at my expense.

'WAWA?' I repeated.

'Yes, a truism if ever there was. West Africa Wins Again, WAWA.'

Then we both laughed.

Just as we landed Bob hit me with a bombshell.

'About that groundnut factory, isn't that where the drunken Russian works?'

Chapter 6
My first job

When I descended the steps of the plane I felt like an overcooked cake on a wire tray. There was no escape from the dry heat. At the same time, it was a relief to get away from the intense humidity of the south. I said my farewell to the informative Bob as he confidently strode off to school. I saw more Muslims in the north and I felt their robes were the best attire for the conditions. Perhaps I'd be more comfortable in one, I thought.

I looked around for just one white face. That would surely be Mr Utechin. I searched in vain. I had to use my initiative. Taxis were very numerous around Tamale airport. They were all yellow and all seemed to be Peugeots. I hailed one.

'Where you go, Masta?' the driver asked.

'The groundnut factory. You know where it is?'

The cab driver looked at me angrily. 'Pioneer Peanuts? You can walk. Look over dere,' he pointed. 'Dat's it,' he said and waved his hand to show he needed a new customer.

I realised the factory was no more than 300 yards away, forming a curtain on one side the runway. I saw that as fortunate for business, then realised that if an aircraft had a shaky landing we might be in the firing line. That was a sobering thought.

I picked up my bags and set off along the red dusty laterite road. I wondered if I would be provided with any transport. Bicycles seemed ubiquitous but I'd only use one for short journeys. The heat was too suffocating.

As I approached the factory, I felt like a schoolboy approaching his new school for the very first time. I knocked on the office door. 'Reception' was written on the frosted glass. It was opened by a native woman.

'Ah, so you are de new manager. We are expecting you,' she said, offering her hand. 'My name is Peace Assare.'

'Peace?'

'Yes, it be my Broffo, I mean my English name.' I nodded. I was beginning to see how different the culture was to anything I had ever known. 'Is Igor Utechin in?' I asked as I looked over her shoulder, anxious to meet the man who would be supervising me.

'De Masta is in but…he is not ready to see you.'

'Oh, I see,' I said slightly confused. 'He is with someone?'

She began to smile and quickly covered her mouth with the back of her hand. 'Come in; sit yourself down by my desk. I go tell you sumthin.'

I pulled up a chair and placed it near her. She was clearly a secretary as well as the receptionist. She sat down opposite me with her typewriter blocking my view of everything but her face.

'You are Mr Utechin's personal secretary?'

'Indeed I am.'

'Then you know who he is with. For how long, I wonder.'

She no longer hid her smile. 'He is with the one he loves. He cannot be disturbed.'

'Ah, his wife is here too?' I asked.

She shook her head from side to side and her shoulders quivered. 'You do not know our Mr Utechin, do you?'

I was confused and disappointed. Yet it seemed she had

30

affection for him. But he had not greeted my arrival. 'No, I know almost nothing about him.'

'He has no wife—as such. One of the local girls go see him some nights. This afternoon he is with his day mistress—as he usually is any time after 3 p.m.'

She must have seen the confusion on my face. Clearly, I had not got her clues and it was a game that needed answers.

'You still no understand? Akpeteshie, it be the local intoxicator. 45% alcohol. That be his true love.'

'That's a lot. Does he not drink vodka or whisky?' I asked remembering what the American Peace Corps teacher had told me.

'He drinks anything, every day, almost anytime. He has udder bottles in his house but de akpeteshie is strong. He likes it the best, fresh from de market.'

So it was true what I had heard as I left the plane. He was a very serious, if not dangerous drinker.

'Then morning is the best time to meet him?'

'Dat be so. It be de only time. Anyway, you no go worry. I take you to your quarters. Der are only de two houses. Yours and Mr. Utechin's.'

We left her office and she clapped her hands. Two young boys appeared and took my bags. They walked ahead of us.

'How long has Mr Utechin been working here?'

'Forever I would say. He looks an old man but I say he be no more than fifty-five, maybe sixty. He's been here since Nkrumah days. President Nkrumah ruled us from 1960 to 1966. Utechin come about 1965 when dey open up de airport. Before, Nkrumah had it for de military. But it had bin a small airport for de War WW2.'

'You liked Nkrumah?' I asked.

'Hmmm he be a fickle man. Americans say he was a communist. He go read about politics and religion an' he want to throw all Europeans out of Africa—dat is except the Russian and udder communist countries. Are you a communist?' she asked me abruptly.

I contemplated my answer for a moment. 'Communist? No, not me.'

'Den I tink we get on well, you an' me here.'

We arrived at a bungalow. It shone white in the daylight like an iceberg. I was clearly its first occupant. Red bougainvillaea surrounded the doorway. Butterflies fluttered away when we approached. A milk bush hedge marked out the garden territory.

'You will have a gardener. His name is Yaw. He keeps de garden in flower, and after de rains he makes sure no snakes are around.'

'Snakes, are the reptiles many?'

'Yes, the rain brings out de snakes. Around here it's usually de Black Cobra.'

'Black Cobra? And can it get into the house?' I asked showing some considerable unease.

Grace laughed. 'They try to get out of your way unless you have some food stuff wif you or you stand on them. You will not be harmed. I assure you,'

A young woman approached. Her age was hard to tell but I guessed she was mid-thirties. She greeted the secretary in her native tongue.

'And this is Amma. She is your servant. She make your meals, cleans de house, washes de clothes, she go shopping for you. She do anyting an' do everything for you, you go understand?'

I smiled at her ambiguity. I was glad to see her baby bound to her back in a coloured cloth. She must have a husband.

'So now I go back to my desk. I see you in de morning. Eight o'clock. I go let you unpack and get settled.'

'Thank you, Peace. You have been very helpful.' And with a spin of her heels, she took off and was out of sight in a matter of seconds.

I entered the new house, still smelling of white painted walls. I walked through the spacious lounge to the kitchen. It seemed to be a magazine picture of knives, tins, fridge and a gleaming cooker too. The bathroom was a shower with a loo. Just enough space to do the necessary washing. There was only one bedroom of ample size and another, no more than a box room. I took my bags to my bedroom and sat down on my bed. I did not know whether to cry at my lack of a greeting from my superior or be delighted by Peace and having both a gardener and a cook/steward.

I unpacked my belongings and hung them up on rails and laid other items in drawers. Having completely unpacked, I got out a pad of paper and sat down to write to Morag.

I began with my Post Box Number—237 Tamale, a simple but adequate address. I was wondering how to start the letter when I heard a knock on the door.

'Agoooo, Hello?'

Amma arrived with a tray on which clinked a glass of ice cubes in some liquid, a slice of lemon and a small bottle labelled 'quinine water'.

I was taken aback. 'Is this for me?' I asked.

'Yes, sir. Your late afternoon drink.'

'But I don't usually have a drink at this time,' I said.

'It is the British way. Gin and quinine to prevent malaria. I thot all white men take dis at dis time.'

I smiled at her. I did not mean to reprimand her. 'I don't need a drink. Anyway, I don't drink spirits.'

'Dat be so? Den I get you a Tata.'

'What's a Tata?'

'It be our local beer. I keep one cool for you in de frig,' she said as her eyes lit up and mine did too.

I smiled broadly. A cool beer was just what I needed to start my letter to Morag.

Chapter 7
Settling into Tamale

The next morning I was eager to get to the office and meet my general manager. After scrambled eggs on toast and two slices of toast with honey, I set off under a sky which was almost azure—except for a few mackerel cloud striations. The sun had been up two hours already, like an insomniac.

I greeted Peace and she told me to wait. Wait I did—for half an hour. In that time I saw her open about two dozen letters and answer the telephone on five occasions. She spoke in her native tongue, leaving me with the impression she was a busy secretary with many social skills and numerous local contacts.

Mr Utechin's door suddenly opened and he strode forward. What struck me first was his Old Testament beard. His walk was unsteady but supported his rotund body. His face was rosy red with blood vessels on show on both his rosy cheeks. He greeted me in Russian. He shook my hand vigorously.

'You have arrived. Good man.' In his hand, he held a round box of chocolates. He held the tin before me.

'Take a couple,' he said with a smile.

I smiled at him and shook my head. 'Sorry, I'm allergic to chocolate.'

'What? All chocolate?'

'Yes. I can eat travel sweets and pastilles and spangles but nothing with chocolate, even hot chocolate as a drink and no chocolate cake either. It sets me off in blisters all over my body, does chocolate.'

'Hmmm, bad luck,' he said launching another unwrapped sweet into his mouth. Then he put the tin down on a desk. His right hand indicated for Peace to enjoy a chocolate. With his left arm, he gestured that he would show me around.

I smiled. 'I'd enjoy that very much,' I said hoping I could gain as much information as necessary about my work before his bewitching hour of bottle consolation.

He was a stocky man too. His complexion was that of an ill alcoholic, beyond any doubt. Perhaps that was why I had to replace him, in time. His brightly coloured flowery Jeromi shirt integrated him into the community. I felt I needed a vibrant shirt like that too. The market should give me a good selection. Shopping for one was something to look forward to.

We entered the huge factory. The heat was immense—despite ventilation gaps in the roof. The first process was the cleaning of the kernels; the outer shell had to be separated from the nut.

'What do you do with the discarded shells?' I asked.

He hitched up his trousers. 'Quite a few uses. Some goats eat them; others are used to start the evening cooking fires, the rest as manure. They decompose quickly.'

I nodded pleased that they had several further uses. In the next compartment was a dated Bulgarian seed processing machine. Its purpose was to crack the nuts then add water to cook them. The water bubbled like the Niagara Falls while the heat made me sweat profusely and the air I breathed seem to roast my throat.

I was relieved to leave that process. I was then taken to the processing workshop where the raw materials came under the screw press. After that, the nut pieces went through a solvent extraction method which made the residual rate of groundnut meal waste below 1%. The rest was groundnut oil and the bottling process went from that point. There was a distribution hut as a separate and securely locked facility at the end of the line.

The tour took the best part of an hour and a half, during which time I found curious eyes on me at every stage. I smiled at the workers, showing some humility. Their response was to show smiles and white teeth as they engaged in the work. Some came forward to shake my hand. They had seen and had met the new manager. They would think I was Russian when I was overheard. And that meant a communist too.

'The only other aspect I'm confused about is how the nuts arrive here in the first place.'

He scratched his ear with his little finger. 'All the ground-nut farmers want me to take their crop. I don't need to seek them. The supply is regular. And there are no unions to interfere with our production.'

'And their wages? Who arranges that?'

'They get paid on delivery. There's a weekly pay for regular employees. Saturdays at mid-day they get paid before they leave work. Peace hands out the cedis. They take their pay like children receiving a birthday present,' he said laughing loudly.

'So, Peace is the receptionist, secretary and accountant?'

'No, she is our secretary, receptionist and she hands out the money which I give her.'

'I see,' I said flicking a female mosquito from feeding on my arm. 'And where will I work?'

Igor pointed towards Peace and informed me there was a room behind her. That was to be my office.

I was impressed with the production of the peanut oil but still wondered what my role was. I asked Igor. He replied in Russian of course. His English was often laboured.

'The sea snake does not move for ages and then, when an unsuspecting victim approaches, it darts out and eats it.'

I reflected on what he meant. Long periods of doing nothing, I assumed. Then hectic moments of activity. That was what I took out of his analogy.

'So when does it get busy?'

'Let's go to your room,' he replied.

We passed Peace without a word and opened the door. There was a large window with glass louvers at a sharp angle to aid air circulation. A roof fan whirled round with blades like dancing dervishes. Underneath was a wooden desk. On it was a pile of letters.

'I'll leave you to get through the correspondence. Some might be addressed to me. Open them anyway and take what action you need to. Peace will keep you right.' As he spoke he turned towards the door. He did not want any more conversation. I let him go.

That was Igor's final instruction. I looked at my watch. It was fast approaching his appointed hour with Bacchus.

I sat down and picked up the letters. I flipped through them. There were seven in total. I dealt with the locally stamped ones first.

The first was from the machine operator in the factory. He was asking if his son could join the firm and replace him one day when he retired or died. I placed the letter aside. I was not sure what vacancy the workforce could offer.

The second was a letter from a local Akpeteshie seller. It was an invoice for Igor—to pay 137 cedis. I had no idea how much 'kill me quick' alcohol that would be. It seemed a lot.

The next two letters were from the airport. They gave the

dates of the flight, the flight numbers and the destinations of the next two batches of boxes of oil.

The fifth letter was a welcome card. It was from Peace. I went to see her to thank her but she was not there. Gone for lunch I presumed.

'Looking for Peace,' I heard a man say as he saw me return to my room.

'Yes, I was.'

'Then you have met her absence.'

I smiled at the antiquated manner in which he spoke. 'I'll see her later. I'm Robert Harvie, the new manager. And you are?'

'Sammy, the maintenance man.'

'Things look very shipshape to me,' I said to please him.

'Shipshape?' he asked bewildered.

'Everything seems in order,' I said turning back to my room having learnt an important lesson.

The last two letters were the most interesting. One had the Russian Embassy logo on the back with an Accra postmark on the front while the other was from London. I opened the latter first. It was from Vasily Chazov. He welcomed me to Tamale and showed his confidence in me. He looked forward to seeing me before too long. That was a tantalising thought. Did it mean next week, next month or when? He also made reference to work, not related to the peanut factory. It was not specific but implied I'd be away from the factory from time to time and that Igor Utechin would understand.

I read and re-read the letter. It seemed Igor had a more significant part to play than I had previously given him credit.

The last letter was from the Russian Embassy in Accra. Once more a welcome note. Everyone seemed to be welcoming me. They also invited me to their embassy and told me a formal invitation would follow soon.

I poured a glass of cold water from the fridge as a knock on the door was heard. I shouted, 'come in,' and a boy appeared with a tray. On it was a bowl of soup and some small bags of roasted nuts. A bunch of bananas were tied to his waist. He also had a bunch of leaves. 'The leaves, are they to eat?'

His response was to laugh. He took from his tray what looked like soggy rice and made it into a ball. He placed it on a leaf and served it to me.

'Kenkey,' he said. 'It be fermented cassava. It come wif dey stew, snail stew. It be good.'

I think he saw my look—should I, or should I not?

'Make you go try dis.'

I nodded.

'So, the kenkey, soup, nuts and banana, how much?'

He gave a look which suggested he knew how much he could get from the white man. 'That be two cedis.'

I gave him three cedis, thanked him for coming and I sat down at my desk to eat. The soup was tasty but the kenkey was a sourdough which I could not swallow with any enjoyment. The snails were surprisingly good if a bit chewy. I had no trouble eating the groundnuts with banana. They went down together well.

When Peace returned she knocked on the door and entered. She smiled. She found me eating. 'It's an acquired taste. Most Europeans don't take to kenkey at first. They prefer fufu. You should try some of dat,' she said lifting the tray. 'Em, how much did you pay for it?'

'You mean everything?'

'Yes, your lunch. The boy would have sold it to you.'

'Yes, he did. Two cedis and a cedi tip I gave him.'

'Two cedis with a cedi dash?' she said raising her voice.

'That's not too much was it?' I asked like an errant schoolboy.

40

'Two cedis is a week's pay for some.'

'Oh, then I won't give him that again.'

'No, no more than 50 pesewa for that meal.' She smiled. She knew I was still on the learning curve.

'Fufu? you said.'

'Yes, it come in different ways. Cassava fufu; plantain fufu, a mixture; I tink you will like dat best. We will be having some at our house dis evening. Come and join us, do please.'

With nothing to do that evening, it was a pleasant thought and I had no hesitation in accepting her kind invitation.

'Will I find your home easily?'

She laughed. 'My husband will pick you up.'

Chapter 8
Ghanaian Hospitality

A large maroon Volvo arrived at my home promptly at 7 p.m. Eric Assare got out of the back seat and shook my hand. He was lean, wearing a short-sleeved blue shirt and grey charcoal trousers. Around his neck, his tie looked like an old school tie. His black hair had gone grey just above both of his ears. He looked around fifty years of age, but that was just a guess.

'I'm very pleased to meet you Mr Harvie. Peace told me you were a fine young man.' He spoke with a refined accent.

'Thank you. She is a very pleasant lady indeed,' I replied as he opened the back door of the car for me to enter. He came round the other side and sat in the back with me. His driver made sure we were seated comfortably before setting off.

'I can't say I'm often in the back seat of a car,' I said but he smiled and tapped his hand on my knee.

'Better not to say that in Ghana. It's the car owner who sits in the back. You are a mere passenger if you sit in the front.'

I nodded slightly. 'I have a lot to learn about Ghanaian life. Are you a native of Tamale?' I asked.

'No, I'm Ashanti, from further south.'

I felt I needed to probe more deeply. 'So, it was work that brought you here,' I said in a matter of fact way.

'There are too many doctors in Kumasi. Anyway, after graduating from King's College Hospital in London I went to the School of Tropical Medicine. I researched West African ailments and traditional medicine. Tamale is more rural. More interesting cases here for me to cure.'

'It's good to hear a doctor say the word cure.'

He nodded. 'In England, they taught me the British way of medicine. I include the African methods too. The inner skin of the pawpaw is an antiseptic, for example. It's used for childhood falls and scrapes as well as motor accidents. Then we have a host of herbal medicine—all of which have their place.'

'It seems you must be able to cure most people then.'

He wiped his brow with a white handkerchief. 'Not so, far from it. There are some illnesses which can't be treated—like severe alcoholism when the patient does not want or can't change his habit.'

'My boss is a bit like that.'

'So Peace tells me. Of course he is also my patient.'

'I see. So, if your list is not too large, perhaps I could join your practice?'

'No problem Mr Harvie. I'll get you registered tomorrow,' he said as the car pulled up before a two storey dwelling with a large garden of flowers at the front.

'What a beautiful garden you have,' I said. It was well lit and colourful.

'I can't show it to you after dark.'

'Why not, is it a superstition?'

He raised his hand and pointed at the back of the garden.

'You see that tree? You see its drooping branches?'

'Over there, yes.'

'They are not branches. They hover over the garbage hole, where things rot easily. It attracts the tree climbing black cobra. You don't want to encounter him.'

'Oh, I see, no I would not like that,' I replied, seeing the night watchman beside the house.

'Goodness, what's he doing?' I asked straining my eyes in disbelief.

'Aruna is gathering his evening meal.'

The watchman was sitting by a Tilley lamp with a large bowl of water in front of him. As flying termites and other insects came, transfixed by the light's attraction, he swooped one hand over them and drowned them. His wife, who was so black I did not see her at first, was sitting by a log fire. A hot flat pan received the insects, where they sizzled in some groundnut oil.

'They eat insects?' I asked with a rising voice.

'Very much so. They are very tasty, crunchy and full of vitamins. I tell you, one day they will catch on in Europe. We will export insects as well as your groundnut oil.' Dr Eric Asare laughed as his eyes rolled at the economic possibilities of his thought.

'Come in Robert,' shouted Peace at the steps of her front door.

'Good evening Peace. Your husband has been giving me a very useful cultural talk.'

She welcomed me into their spacious lounge. Wooden carvings on the wall and a traditionally woven floor carpet gave it a homely atmosphere.

We talked about Eric's time after London and how he met Peace. They had met at a gospel evening in Kumasi, thirty-eight years ago. My eyes turned to a sleeping baby in a cot in the corner of the room.

'That's Yaw, my grandson. His parents have travelled,' she said without telling me where.

It was not long before I had to explain my route to Tamale. I think they were surprised it had started so long ago, and on holiday on a Scottish island, but Eric could see how I found myself entrapped in the Russian net.

'Have you met, Mr Frempong?' asked Peace.

'Frempong? I don't think so. '

'He's the man in charge of the shelling process.'

'Oh, now I know who you mean. I have not spoken to him yet.'

Peace gave her husband a sly look. Was she about to say too much? That look was in her eyes. 'He's an old-timer, as it were.'

Her remark made no impact on my thinking.

'He was an Nkrumah man, a communist. One who has worked in the factory since the day the Russians arrived to run it.'

My frown brought my eyebrows together tightly. I was confused. 'But Kwame Nkrumah was the first black African leader. He was the first President of Ghana when the Gold Coast was no more. 'That was surely an achievement of note?'

Eric smiled. 'It was and we can't take that away from him. But he became President not because he got on with the British but because he didn't.'

'What do you mean?'

'Robert, the British ran their colonies through indirect rule. The French were more direct in their approach. They even sent black politicians to sit in parliament in Paris. But the British ruled through the chiefs. They kowtowed to the chiefs and serviced them with gifts, and so gained tribal loyalties. They sent the chief's sons and daughters to England to school and university. But Nkrumah was a Roman Catholic, not a chief. He came from a small western village and was seen as a revolutionary upstart. He was eventually imprisoned,' Eric looked at me with a stern face.

'Not the best route to become President,' I suggested.

'Well maybe not. When he was released, he promised the market women of the country better conditions and they unanimously followed him through the elections. He won a landslide victory. The market women secured that.'

'I see,' I said as I finished the Tata beer I had been given.

'The British came on their knees to congratulate him but Nkrumah was having none of it. His support was now coming from Moscow. Ever since then, Frempong has been besotted by Russia and communism.'

'Wow what a history lesson,' I said uncrossing my legs.

'Come to de table boys,' said Peace' as her servant Seth, produced a large pot of groundnut soup and sat it in the middle of the table. On each of our plates, a mass of what looked like putty settled with a shiver. They caught me eyeing my plate.

'That's fufu. Boiled and pounded cassava and plantain. There are chicken pieces in the groundnut soup—I know Europeans enjoy eating this.'

'But first, let me say grace,' said Eric in a more sombre tone. Peace and I bowed our heads.

'We thank you, Lord, for new friendships made, to meet in harmony and enjoy each other's company. We give thanks for this food on the table, dear Lord. Make it serve our physical needs to sustain us in thoughtful prayer. And with this meal, put it to our use and us to thy service. This we ask in your name, Amen.'

Peace repeated the Amen and I followed a moment later, a little quieter. Then the soup was poured over the fufu. I noticed I had a spoon but neither Peace nor Eric had one. As I lifted my utensil, they dipped their right hands into the soup gathering some fufu as they did. In one quick movement, it slipped down their throats. They saw me chew the fufu and laughed.

'Take a small amount with the soup and swallow it straight away. We do not chew it.'

It was such a filling meal that I soon felt bloated and

ready to sleep. Thoughtfully, an hour later they brought the evening to an end, and when I returned to bed I dreamt of the hospitality I had received, together with the history lesson.

I also dreamt about meeting Mr Frempong. Was he an active collaborator with his Russian boss, or just a sleeper to be used when it suited the powers in Moscow—or perhaps in Accra? I had experience of just how long they could wait.

When I woke my thoughts became more realistic. Nkrumah's day was over and the Russians had given me a job with no strings attached, surely?

Chapter 9
Secret Ashes

By the third week at the factory I seemed to have understood every part of the oil production process. Farmers regularly brought in their peanut harvest and were paid promptly, which pleased them. The machinery was itself oiled and working well to chaff the shells, and the press brought out the oil to where sterile bottles were filled every day. Lorries stood in a line at the end of the premises to transport the bottles in cartons of 12 to the airport, a stone's throw away. It was a slick business model.

I was sitting at my desk when I began to smell burning. I stood up and headed towards the glass louvers to locate the source of this nasal intrusion. I saw outside Mr Frempong standing over a brazier. He seemed to be in a daze. He was throwing paper by the handful into the hungry flames from a box. With a wooden stick, he turned over the pages, ensuring they completely burned.

If these were his own papers then he should not have been using up company time to burn them, but I thought they must be work-related and so I decided to investigate for myself. I made my way out of the building wondering how to challenge Mr Frempong politely.

When I turned around the corner of the office, I saw

the conflagration had died down and there was no sign of anyone. The box had gone.

The stick Mr Frempong had used lay beside the brazier. I approached feeling the heat warm my face. I lifted the stick and flicked out a few half-burnt pages and stood on them. I picked up the first, which stunned me into retrieving more from the embers. In the end, I saved four pages that had artistically burnt edges. I spread them out on the ground. They were lists. I ordered them alphabetically. They were the names and addresses of most of the National Embassies in Accra, the capital. Some had lines drawn through them while others had an asterisk beside the name or the address.

I held them gingerly in case they would further disintegrate and returned to my office. I did not quite reach the door.

Peace sat smiling, waving a blue paper. 'It's airmail for you,' she said thrusting her hand towards me with the correspondence.

'Airmail?' I queried. I asked Peace if Moscow had an instruction for me.

'Yes, airmail, try again. Think more personal. I mean think of a fluttering heart,' she giggled like a school girl.

I had forgotten how she had grilled me during the delightful evening at her home about the girl I'd left behind in Scotland. It dawned on me—of course, Morag must have written. I took the letter from her and turned it over, and in seeing the return address my thoughts were confirmed.

'I'll bring you a coffee and see that you are not disturbed.'

I smiled and thanked her, but her expression turned to disgust. 'I think you should wash your hands first. Goodness knows how you have got dem so dirty.'

After hurriedly washing my hands, I sat down at my desk. I took a knife to carefully slice open the feather-light aerogramme. I turned it over to read the last line and a smile appeared on my face. Morag had written of her undying love and smothered the last line with a row of hugs and kisses. I had been forgiven. I launched into reading her letter with a hungry appetite for her news.

Of course, to begin with, she responded to the points I had made in my letter to her. She had acknowledged it had arrived ten days after I posted it. The main point of her letter was that she was getting her yellow fever injection the following week, and in a month's time, she would be in Ghana at the Korle Bu teaching hospital's maternity unit. I checked the date the letter was written. That meant in twenty days she would be in Accra. I had to see Utechin soon about some leave.

Now I had two reasons to speak to him. Would he be in a generous mood if I approached him right away? I looked at my watch. It was almost 3 p.m.—I'd have to wait until tomorrow.

Chapter 10
Morag gets a mention

I woke early to another inevitably dry scorching day. I had already decided, having slept on it, to bring up the subject of Morag first and hope for a benevolent response. Utechin was likely to be touchier about his list of embassies.

As he passed through the office, I signalled him over.

'Could I have a moment or two of your time this morning? I have a couple of questions you could help me with.'

'There's no time like the present, Robert,' he said, pointing to his office. I stood up and followed him through his door, shutting it behind me. He opened all the glass louvers, though I could not feel any breeze as it slowly made its way inside the room. A carafe of what I presumed was akpeteshie sat on a silver tray near the door

'Have a seat and tell me what's bothering you,' he said in his guttural Russian.

I took a deep breath as I sat down. 'I am not sure if you know I have a girlfriend.'

'You are young. Of course, you have many girlfriends. At your age it can't be serious—not so? Anyway, it's easy to pick up a local girl. They love sex with the white man,' he laughed as his eyes turned towards the ceiling and moments of passion seemed to fill his mind.

I cracked my knuckles at his response. 'No, I don't have lots of girlfriends. Just the one and she is training to be a doctor. That is why I need to talk to you.'

'Ah Robert, you are worried about my drinking. Is that the advice she is giving you to pass on to me?'

I smiled, mainly to hear his acknowledgement of his alcoholic guilt. 'No, she will soon be spending six weeks working at the Korle Bu teaching hospital in Accra.'

The atmosphere chilled. I could almost see his thoughts at work behind his dark eyebrows. 'I wonder if I could have some leave—to see her?'

'I see. Leave that with me for a couple of days. I'll see what I can do. Now you had another matter.'

The thought that my leave had not been finalised worried me. Was I about to lose all leave while Morag was in Accra? But I had to put that to one side as he asked about my second issue.

'I noticed a burning smell yesterday. It was outside at the back.'

'Ah yes, just burning a few papers. They make good compost, the ash, you know?'

I could feel my heart beat rapidly as I struck home. 'I managed to save a few pages. They was a list of embassy addresses in Accra.'

He smiled at me. He was certainly not angry.

'Yes, a list as you say. Of many friendly countries like Romania, Poland, and Czechoslovakia—and some who bother us, like the USA, Canada, Australia, South Africa etc.'

I noticed he did not mention the UK.

'Russia is always under threat from the West. We have a superior political system to theirs but they don't agree with us. We have to defend the fatherland and attack our enemies—as we did in World War 2. That is why we have a list. I had made a new list with the latest information I had. I asked Frempong to burn the old list.'

He had provided a robust response, but I could not see how he was involved. 'This seems like the work of an embassy, not a peanut factory, surely?'

I waited for his response. He sat forward, placed his arms on the table and interlocked his fingers. 'The Russian embassy is our head office. This peanut factory is our cover in the north.'

'Our cover? In what way?' I asked with indecent haste, anxiety and surprise.

'On Ghana's northern frontier is Upper Volta, a former French colony, soon to be an independent country. Eighty per cent of the people are Muslim and the rest mainly Christian—and then there are the nomads, the Tuareg.'

'The Tuaregs, you mean the ones who wander all over the Sahara?'

He smiled at me. 'Yes, they follow the seasons, but it's a regular pattern. When they arrive in Tamale in the dry season, during the harmattan, I meet with them.'

I was still confused. 'Why?'

'Propaganda, my boy, propaganda. Make them believe in the greatness of motherland Russia.'

'But how?'

'By identifying their leaders and offering them opportunities to study in Moscow. You know, just like we paid for your study in Glasgow.'

This was the first time Utechin had mentioned my links as a student. I felt uneasy with his knowledge of my past.

'So—you have the Tuareg eating out of your hands?'

'Too simple, Robert. Patience is the word. There's no need to rush.'

On that, I agreed with him. I felt I had much to consider. I'd prise him open at another time.

'Well, I had better get back to my desk.'

'You do that, Robert. We can talk another day,' he said with sincerity, but his eyes were already on the carafe on the sideboard.

Chapter 11
The Enigmatic Amadu

I was leisurely answering some work correspondence at my desk two mornings later. As I sipped a black coffee Utechin barged into my room and stood before me. His smile was as large as the Volta Lake.

'Got you working in Accra for six weeks, while your girl-friend is down there.'

I put down my pen sat back with a smile and my arched eyebrows begged him to give me further news.

'You will be staying in the airport area—where all the embassies are. You will be living in the Russian Embassy and they will find work for you.'

'Wow, I can't thank you enough. But being away for six weeks, how will the work get done here?'

He pouted his lips. 'You can't say it's a taxing post, can you?'

'No, not really but the temperatures make any work much harder.'

He nodded briefly. Then he lit a cigarette. 'I'll tell Peace. She can cover for you. She's a good hard worker.'

When he had gone I moved the correspondence to one side and took out an aerogramme. I wrote to inform Morag about this change of circumstances. She was bound to be pleased.

Amadu was a Tuareg. There could be no mistaking him in his flowing light blue robes and white scull cap. I saw him approach, coming out of the haze as if in a film. That meant the dry, dusty harmattan was on its way. It would prove to be a mixed blessing. It lowered the searing temperatures a bit, but at times visibility was also reduced dramatically. It cast a veil of red dust on every flat surface in my house and on my work desk. The dry dust-laden atmosphere made catarrh clog my lungs, resulting in frequent nose blowing.

Amadu looked up through the louvers of my window. He bowed. I waved. I knew I had better introduce myself promptly, and made my way to meet him.

'Salaam Alaikum,' I said as I stretched out my hand in welcome. He smiled at me and responded appropriately. His accent surprised me. He spoke with what seemed to be a European accent, which confused me. My ears went on alert.

'How are you enjoying Ghana,' he asked.

'It's much warmer than Scotland,' I said to him with a broad smile. 'I'm sure you can't imagine how cold it is in my country.'

'I know how cold things can be. Especially, when I fly.' His smile engaged me.

'Cold—when you fly? I don't understand.'

'Cold, when I learned to fly.'

'You mean you are a pilot?' I said with a doubting glance.

He smiled. 'Yes, I was trained by Hanna Reitche. She was a supporter of Hitler. She was invited to Ghana by Kwame Nkrumah and she lived here from 1962 to 1966. She taught me to fly.'

I tried not to show my total amazement that this elegantly robed African was a pilot. But I was still intrigued. 'What planes do you fly?'

'I learned to fly a double-seated Schleicher K7—and a

Slingsby T21. They are gliders. But I also learned to fly a Piper Cherokee 150.'

'That's impressive. So, where do you fly?'

He laughed. 'From here!' and he pointed to the airport nearby.

'So, you have your own plane?'

'Of course.'

He caught my obvious disbelief. 'But I thought you are a nomadic Tuareg?'

'Yes, but not all the time. Sometimes I work for Mr Utechin.'

I hesitated. It explained his presence but gave no other hint.

'I did not know you worked in the peanut oil industry.'

His smile showed two rows of beautiful white teeth. 'No, not for the factory. I am his eyes,' he said raising his eyebrows.

'Can I call you a spy, then?' I joked.

He approached me and grabbed my hand. He gave me a quick shake then he snapped our thumbs together before giving me a final handshake. It seemed to confirm my suspicions.

I was sitting at my desk checking the supply of raw peanuts when Mr Utechin appeared and invited me into his office. Peace was gathering some papers in his room.

I stood still. My eyes looked over to Peace. She pouted her lips. She had no idea why I had been summonsed either.

As soon Peace left the room, the door was closed and he spoke in Russian.

'Before you head down to Accra, I have a job for you, which I am sure you will enjoy.'

I was glad to have a break from the monotony of the work and I eagerly listened to what he had in mind.

'Amadu will fly you to Sandema. It's not a long trip. It is north-west of here by a hundred miles or so. It's a village hardly a tenth of Tamale, but there is a presence of some Spanish people. You speak Spanish fluently, don't you?'

'Er…yes, it was one of my specialities at university.'

'Good. There is one man there. His name is Lorenzo. Lorenzo Desoto. He will be easy to identify. He has a Russian accent.'

'I see,' I said not really understanding why this man had a Spanish name. Utechin caught my uncertainty.

'You can say he is double-disguised. When he retired from our government service as a petrochemical engineer he took on a Spanish name. It helped him to find work in this Spanish enterprise. He used to work in Madrid, but yes, he's Russian.'

Mr Utechin opened a drawer and brought out a paper-wrapped box. He handed it over to me.

'A box of chocolates. He is one of us, a Russian, a very useful individual doing some very good work.'

'Do I need a cover? I presume I need one?'

'You tell him you have a present from Alfonso.'

'And who is Alfonso?'

'Alfonso works in Accra. He is the managing director of this project in Sandema. They have met on a few occasions. They seem to be good friends.'

'I see, so how long will I be in Sandema?'

'You find Lorenzo; give him the box of chocolates. Be polite. Remember they came from his friend in Accra. No need to talk about Tamale, your work here or me. Tell him you are a traveller. You met Alfonso – he's six-foot tall, thin with short black hair, in Accra and he asked you to give this package to his friend as you were heading up to the Upper Volta border. Then, as soon as you can, you fly back to Tamale with Amadu.'

'I see and when do you want me to go?'
'Tomorrow is a good day.'

That night I lay awake in my bed going over my instructions—deliver a box of chocolates to a Russian spy disguised as a Spaniard and beat my way back to Tamale as soon as I can. I was confident of what was expected of me and I guessed the box of chocolates signalled to Lorenzo Desoto that he was doing a good job. In effect, it was a message saying 'well done'. To the hum of the ceiling fan, sleep overcame me.

When I woke the following morning, I had a spring in my step. A short flight, a simple task and back in daylight for sure. What could possibly go wrong?

Chapter 12
A Mission to Sandema

Amadu told me he had been at his plane since six that morning when I strolled up at half-past seven. He had rolled up his long gown and was sitting with headphones on in a slender looking double-seated craft.

'Salaam Alaikum, Robert,' he said waving me onboard behind him.

'Alaikum Salaam,' I replied. 'Is there an airport near Sandema?'

He seemed to think that was a huge joke. 'No...no no no. The land is flat and hard,' he replied, his shoulders still shaking in mirth. 'That's all this plane needs.'

My thoughts turned to a painfully bumpy landing, but I knew he must have flown to many such runways and I placed my trust in him.

A thumb up from the conning tower was reciprocated by Amadu and we taxied down the runway to one end. He made a final check of his instruments. I hoped he had checked the fuel in particular—but who was I to question the pilot, indeed any pilot?

Then the race along the runway began. I felt like a fit ostrich running along the tarmac until the nose of the plane lifted and my seat seemed to drop. In no time at all we were seeing the mud huts of outer Tamale laid out in a regular pattern, like sporadic buttons on an orangey-red laterite cardigan. There were hungry vultures perched on the acacia trees seeking any overnight carcass. The coloured cloths of the women bearing heavy weights on their heads as they returned from the market grew smaller.

The flight was only forty minutes or so. As we descended I had my eyes peeled for a regular landing area initially, but the nearness of the trees made me concentrate on their avoidance. With no more than a slight light bump or two, the wheels soon took over and with a wobble, we sped along the flat dusty ground. Amadu brought the plane to a halt under a spreading acacia tree.

I soon realised just how much shade the plane was enjoying—as soon as I was in the open, the temperature soared to what must have been over 110 degrees. I wore a Bolgatanga hat, which had a very wide rim and was made of straw. I had seen so many farmers wearing them that I knew I almost looked compatible from a distance. It served its purpose well.

'So, where do I return to be collected, Amadu?'

'I stay beside my plane to keep unwelcome eyes from investigating it. I'll be here when you return. Master says you won't be very long.'

'That's good. But where is the factory? In the town? How far away is it?'

Amadu turned some forty-five degrees around and pointed at a compound, which included a tower, some considerable distance away. 'That's where the Spanish are working.'

I shook his hand. His information was invaluable and I looked forward to my return trip more than the mundane assignment before me. It seemed strange. Hand over a box of chocolates and return. Why not post them from Accra? Perhaps it was so that I might get to know the Russian

Spaniard, Lorenzo? Perhaps chocolates in the post might never reach the recipient. Maybe they would have melted long ago had not Igor kept them in his fridge. I could not answer my own questions.

I must have walked for fifteen minutes as the metal tower grew larger by each step. The sweat no sooner left me than it dried instantly, and soon I needed some water. I drank as if taking my last drink ever and quickly finished my bottle.

As I approached I saw a few trucks and several stationary jeeps. There were four buildings. But first, there was a security gate. I approached. I wondered if it was best to speak French or Spanish, but first I extended my hand and exchanged an Islamic greeting with the man on duty.

'I've come to speak to Senor Lorenzo Desoto.'

'Ah...Senor Desoto. Yes, he be here.'

I smiled at him and nodded, indicating I knew he would be here. 'Where do I go find him, please?'

He pointed at the second hut from the left. 'He dey work in dat room.'

I shook his hand warmly and proceed past the makeshift security gate. I approached the wooden door of the hut and knocked three times.

'Come in,' a voice said and immediately I detected a southern Russian accent in his Spanish tongue. I entered and found a slightly nervous, underweight man with a well-bronzed face and greying hair which may have been red at one time. It seemed the heat did not suit him.

'Good morning, my name is Robert Harvie,' I said in Spanish, then proffered the parcel and explained that I had met Alfonso in Accra, that I was his messenger delivering this present.

Lorenzo relaxed but no smile came to his lips. He took the box and laid it on his table. He eyed me knowing I, like him, spoke Spanish with a different European accent.

I could see the moment was becoming uncomfortable for him. Then he began to question me.

'How do you know Alfonso?'

'I met him at the Osu beach, near Accra.'

'How exactly did you meet?' he asked. His manner reminded me of an irritated school teacher.

'Well, it's an interesting story,' I began. 'I studied Spanish when I was at school and university. As I lay on the beach I overheard two men speaking Spanish. I presumed they were from the cargo ships at either Tema, along the coast, or further away at Sekondi-Takoradi.' That did not end his enquiry and he sat back to hear more.

'So I was glad to practice my Spanish with them in Accra of all places. One of them turned out to be Alfonso. He asked why I was in Ghana I told him I was going to see the whole country. I said I was first heading to Tamale, then to Navrongo and up to Upper Volta. That was when he told me he had a friend called Lorenzo Desoto and he would arrange for me to bring you something. He came to where I was staying at a rest house in Accra with this box, and so now I am here, to present you with his gift.'

He seemed to accept my lie, which I found uncomfortably easy to deliver. After a few moments, his smile reappeared. 'You speak Spanish well.'

His shoulders relaxed. Tension left him.

'I saw a tower on my approach. What's the work here?' I asked, hoping to change the subject.

He stood up and walked over to the window, lowering the slanted louvers at an angle for a view through the mosquito netting. 'Come over here and see.'

'Over there, Mr Harvie, you see they are drilling?' he asked.

I kept my Spanish simple. 'Drilling,' I repeated in surprise.

'Yes, for oil.'

'So, there is oil under the sand here?'

'There's oil in Libya and only the desert lies between us. We are hopeful.'

He returned to his desk and brought out a map of West Africa. 'See Libya here? Sandema here,' his finger ran between the two points. 'Sand and oil, nothing more, nothing less.'

'Aha,' I said, hoping I showed sufficient enthusiasm for his project. He returned to his desk after closing the glass louvers and increased the speed of the ceiling fan en route. He began to unpack the box. Inside was a tin of Quality Street chocolates. He took out a knife and cut around the sellotape, freeing the lid. I saw his eyes light up at the sight of chocolates. He lifted one. He felt it. 'I think I'd better put them in the fridge for an hour or two.'

There was no need to inform him of my chocolate allergy. I agreed they would be better chilled. To change the subject I asked a favour. 'I'd appreciate refilling my water bottle,' I said.

'Yaw,' he shouted and before I understood why the door opened.

'Yaw, take this box and put it in the fridge. And can you take my friend's water bottle and refresh it?' he asked his steward.

'Yes master, I go do this,' he said and left as soon as he had appeared.

'So, where are you heading now, can I ask?'

A true answer was not in my mind. Fortunately, I knew the names of some of the towns nearby. 'I'll stay in Navrongo tonight. I know a teacher there.'

'Navrongo, that's not too far.'

'Yes, I know. I'll get a lorry from Sandema. I have an American friend, a mathematics teacher there.'

Yaw entered the room once more with two new bottles of water for me. I thanked him profusely.

'Then my driver can take you to Navrongo.'

'That would be great,' I said smiling at his thoughtfulness. Then I wondered how I would get back to Sandema, the plane and home.

'Well, enjoy your chocolates. I'll be on my way.'

'Sorry about them. Perhaps I can give you a few. They might even have started to set already.'

'No, that's alright. Best to have them solid and enjoy all of them.'

He was having none of it. He went out of the room but kept the door open. He returned with a brown paper bag with four wrapped chocolates inside.

'Enjoy them.'

'I certainly will. I'll have them in the car and enjoy the journey more.' There was no need for a lengthy explanation about my allergy—I recalled Igor's words to deliver and depart.

Lorenzo went to the door and shouted for his car. 'Well Mr Harvie, it has been a pleasure meeting you. Perhaps we can meet again?'

'One thing I meant to ask you Senor Desoto. Do you still speak much Russian?'

'Could you detect I am Russian?'

'I thought you had a slight Russian accent. But you are working with the Spanish?'

'It pays to be bilingual doesn't it, Mr Harvie?'

Before I could ask more questions of this most enigmatic man, he announced the car was waiting outside. He proffered his hand and I shook it firmly.

I had got used to sitting in the back of cars, as all Europeans and wealthy Ghanaians did to show they were the car's owner, even if they weren't. In no time at all, I had passed Amadu, who was resting beside his plane. I was glad he did not see me. I saw the lorry park in the village and told the driver to stop there. I told him I'd like to go on one of the wooden lorries to Navrongo. To travel like a native, I said. It would impress my teacher friend.

'Ah, you mean the tro-tro?'

'Yes, that's the name I've heard people call it.'

'Tro-tro—it means tuppence, tuppence. It's the cheap way to travel. You will find yourself squashed between several market women,' he said as he stopped at the entrance to the lorry park.

I thanked him and he offered to stay with me till the lorry came, but I assured him that was not necessary. As he drove off I made my way into Sandema town. As I passed a family outside their home, lighting a fire to boil water, I stopped and took out from my pocket the bag with the four wrapper covered chocolates. I approached the children and gave them each one. Their smiles were gigantic, as was their mother's in showing her appreciation.

Then I made my way back towards Amadu and his plane. It was such a reassuring sight and I was pleased when the wheels left the ground and Sandema and even Navrongo disappeared from sight. I looked at the land far below with a hint of satisfaction. My cover seemed secure. Yet it had been such a simple task. Delivering Quality Street from someone I knew only by description.

Once we landed I thanked Amadu and gave him some cedis for all his efforts in assisting me. As it was still only 3.30 p.m. I made my way back to the office, but of course, only Peace was there to greet me.

'How did you enjoy Sandema?' she asked.

'It seemed hotter than here and that's saying something.'

She laughed. 'What were you doing there?' she enquired, curiosity in her eyes.

'Delivering chocolates. That's about it.'

She looked glum. 'There's rarely a box of chocolates in this office.'

'Perhaps I can address that. Is the boss…' I cut short the sentence and finished it with a shaking finger to my lips.

Peace nodded. 'Obliterated, as usual.'

Chapter 13
Nkansa's true Colours

The next morning Igor Utechin sought me out first thing.

'Robert, how did it go?'

'Quite well, I think.'

'Were you offered any chocolates?'

'Yes, I was,' I said.

'You didn't eat any did you?' he asked taking me by surprise.

'No, I told you I was allergic to chocolate. But as they were so soft; he put them in the fridge.'

A smile came over Utechin's face. I was unsure why, but he seemed pleased that I had not taken one. Over-concerned I thought. He knew I had an allergy to them.

'He did offer me some when I was leaving, but I thought it best to tell him I'd have them in the car on my way back.'

'And did you? Or did you give them to the driver?' he asked in haste.

'Of course not. I told you they make me ill. I actually gave them to a family with four children. You can imagine how pleased and surprised they were. They couldn't get the wrappers off quickly enough,' I said recalling the moment with great satisfaction—but Utechin seemed out of sorts. I turned to head towards my desk after he failed to ask any more questions. He seemed deep in thought. Perhaps his hangover was particularly bad.

He followed me into my office.

'Robert, you are in charge for the time being. I'll be in hospital for tests for a couple of days.'

'Nothing serious I hope?'

'Time will tell young man. Time will tell.'

Around mid-day, there was knock on the door.

'Come in,' I shouted looking up. 'Ah Mr Nkansa, what can I do for you this morning?'

He looked humble, holding his hat in both hands on his lap when he sat down.

'It be our pay. We've not had a rise for a while.'

'I see. Well that's a matter for Mr Utechin, when he comes back from hospital.'

Nkansa looked around the room furtively. I had never seen him in my room before. I awaited his response, my pen tapping my knee out of his sight.

'Mr Utechin, he's an ill man.'

'Yes, I can see dat.'

Another pause—but this time I saw him fight for his words.

'Will you…er… take over from Mr Utechin?' he asked, looking at me directly

'That's a bit premature, surely?'

'I don't tink so, or I would not have asked.'

'Okay, you have asked a decent question. The answer is that I really don't know. If I left then the powers that be could appoint someone from here, I am sure. But we are not at that stage, I assure you.'

Mr Nkansa nodded for a moment. He had exhausted that topic.

'A pay rise then?' he asked with tilt of his head.

'Is this just you asking, or on behalf of your workmates?'

'We have formed a union. I am the secretary and I speak for the members.'

I held my chin in my hand. 'I see. And how many members do you have?'

'We have five at present, but more will join.'

'Five? That's not even half the workforce. But I am sympathetic. I'll tell you what I'll do. When Mr Utechin returns, it will be the first point on my agenda. I promise to let you know how we will proceed with your request. Is that fair?'

He pondered my suggestion. Then I saw a slight nod of his head.

'Yes, that be fair,' he said moving the chair back before standing up.

'Just a moment Mr Nkansa. You were a Nkrumah supporter. Are you still of that view?'

'Nkrumah, for all his faults was de first black African leader. He is the flame which lights our continent. You can't take that away from him.'

'You are right—I can't and don't want to. But he is no longer leader. Things move on, we have to adjust.'

'We move on yes, but don't forget the past. Nkrumah brought the Russians here. They helped us stand on our own two feet after independence. The British drifted away.'

I nodded—he spoke the truth, as I knew it to be.

'Even today, I see Russia as my friend. I am happy to work under Mr Utechin.'

'Then I suspect he will hear your proposition fairly.'

Nkansah rightly took that as the end of our encounter. He offered his hand.

'By the way, when you were in Sandema, did you see Mr Desoto?'

'Er...yes, I met him?' I said wondering how he knew about Desoto.

'Did he take the chocolates?'

My mind was in turmoil. Why did Utechin quiz me so

intently about the chocolates, and now Mr Nkansa? Were they in some plot together?

'Yes, he took them,' I said, watching to gauge his response. It was a smile.

'Fine,' he said and left without a further word.

Chapter 14
I Must Leave Tamale

Two days later I saw a car drive up outside the office. As the passenger's door opened the first thing I saw was a walking stick. Utechin followed and stood with its aid. Then I saw Peace go out to support him and bring him into the building. She returned to the car and took the day's edition of the *Ghanaian Times* newspaper from the back seat. I waited until he was settled in his office chair before I went to inquire after his health.

His back was to me as I entered. 'How are you feeling?' I asked in Russian.

He turned around with no hint of a smile. His hand was shaking and then he thumped the table. 'We've got to get you to Accra as soon as possible, Robert.'

'Why?' I blurted. 'What's the rush?'

He grabbed the *Ghanaian Times* and threw it at me.

I picked it up. The headline struck me to my core.

FOUR CHILDREN DEAD
POISONED BY SWEETS IN SANDEMA

I read on with shaking hands and total disbelief. "A white man gave some chocolates to them," said their grieving mother. My hands still shook and a lump formed in my throat. My description had been given to the police who were also looking into a death at an oil company compound, where a Senor Lorenzo Desoto had also died in similar circumstances, from poisoning. The authorities had requested additional police from Kumasi to be drafted in to solve the five murders. There was a fear that there might be more deaths waiting to be uncovered.

'But…but…I had no idea the chocolates were poisonous. They looked like ordinary Quality Street Sweets. The police must know that, I should tell them,' I said with indignation as the implication of being a mass murderer hit home.

'You are involved in five murders Robert – four of them of children – but the country is behind you. That is why we must get you to Accra and the Russian embassy as soon as possible.'

I felt a coolness come over me despite the rising heat. I had been used to kill a man, and that had resulted in four further deaths. Of children.

'But why kill Lorenzo?' I asked in bewilderment.

'He was a spy who defected. He had to pay the price. You did a good job there. It was just unfortunate that you gave those chocolates to the children. Now get packed—you must leave this afternoon. Understand?'

Understand I did but I thought that if I had only been told the contents of the tin I would never have given those chocolates to the children. On the other hand, if I knew the sweets had been tampered with, I might never have gone to Sandema. Sweets? Of course, Utechin knew I was allergic to chocolate. So did Chazov in London. It came back clearly to me now.

'Peace, get Amadu over here quick,' Utechin shouted and I felt no urge to inquire further of his health.

I returned to my house in haste and packed up everything I could take. I left a box of tissues and a novel, *The*

Parrot's Tale, which I had read. Goodness knows whose hands it would find itself in, but I hoped they would enjoy it as much as I had.

Utechin's occasional driver came to collect me and my two bags and drove me the short distance to the airport. I recognised the aeroplane and then saw Amadu appear from the other side of his aircraft.

'A longer flight this time,' he said with a grin.

I knew he had been told of the need to get me out of Tamale as soon as possible. Perhaps he did not know why.

'Yes, Accra. Another smooth flight?'

'I hope so. Built-up areas, more air traffic. We've got to go over the Kwahu ridge too. Need some height for that. But for you, some spectacular Ghanaian jungle to admire.'

A few minutes later we were taxiing along the runway once more. Then thumbs up again and the race along the runway began.

Only when the wheels left the ground and tucked themselves into the body of the plane could I start to physically relax. My body went limp. My mind was however in overdrive. To some, I would just seem foolish getting into this mess, but I knew others would be on my tail, seeking a mass murderer.

I wondered what could I expect from the Russian embassy? I thought I would be able to see Morag more—I realised she would be in Accra in a week or two. A letter to her that night would be a priority. But how much could I tell her? God, what a mess I was in.

I was met at Kotoka International Airport in Accra by a car bearing the Corps Diplomatique insignia. The driver took my bag and placed it in the boot. With almost indecent haste he pushed me into the back of the car in such a way I wondered if I had been kidnapped. When I got my bearings, I realised the windows were blacked out.

'Are we heading to the Russian Embassy?' I asked for clarification, holding on to the back of the driver's seat.

'Yes, sir. They are expecting you.'

In those six words, I felt a growing sense of satisfaction. I would be safe for the time being, and if the coast was clear I'd have Morag to comfort me once more.

The drive was short. Embassy residences were near the airport in the residential district of the city. The car went up the drive and round the back of the residence, where it pulled into in a demarcated parking space.

As I got out of the car, a man greeted me.

'Welcome Robert, I am Vitaly Karmanov, First Secretary. I am glad you have arrived safely.'

His smile disarmed me. I returned my thanks for his welcome in Russian.

'Come, let me take you to your room.'

I followed on as we entered the residence and climbed the stairs at the back. It led to a corridor and at its end, a door. He opened it and I stepped into a large square room with a view of the garden at the rear. It seemed the foliage went on forever.

'This is where you will be for the time being.'

'The time being?' I said, wondering how long I would have to be here.

'Enough time for you to grow a beard, enjoy the facilities of the residence and relax. There will also be some debriefing required, of course.'

'Grow a beard?' I said in astonishment. But it was not a request. 'Of course,' I replied out of instinct. I must not put a foot wrong. A disguise would help me.

'You will eat with the Russian staff in the rear dining room. I need not tell you that all correspondence will be checked before posting. That means diplomatic bag dispatches as well as local mail, so don't seal your letters.'

I nodded, showing my understanding.

'There is a bell system in your room. Use it freely, but only contact the ambassador in extremis. Your requests will be answered by me or one of the other staff.'

'Thank you. So—I'll unpack and settle in,' I said, feeling I was secure in this protected place, yet wondering how they might use me.

'Am I confined to barracks, as it were? No leaving the residence?'

'Exactly, but do use the swimming pool—you'll find it at the rear, or the tennis court. There will be plenty of opposition for you, both Russian staff and domestic, as well as the Ghanaian secretarial staff.'

He must have felt I had received enough information for the time being. I noticed a shower in an adjoining room and a wash hand basin. That was what I needed to calm my nerves, a warm shower.

I opened my toilet bag and took out my razor and laid it to one side. I had a look at myself in the mirror. I saw a man ill at ease. A man on the run from murder and that gnawing feeling increased each day. Would I be betrayed? Could I ever live without this guilt? A man trapped with no apparent exit. A man longing for his girlfriend to calm his worries. A man with a growing stubble.

Chapter 15
Life at the Russian
Embassy in Accra

Shortly after noon there was a knock on the door. Two Ghanaians appeared. Dressed in formal white trousers and jackets, the contrast with their skin was startling. One had a tray with two sandwiches, a bottle of water, an orange and a banana. The other brought a multi colourer towel with him.

'For a swim this afternoon, after you have eaten, sir,' said the towel bearing servant.

'All other lunches will be downstairs, but today, the lunch tray is here for you,' said the other.

Then they departed. I did not even ask their names. There was so much on my mind.

I enjoyed the meal, simple as it was, and wondered if the evening meal might be more formal. Then I unrolled the swimming towel to discover a pair of swimming trunks. They were not new, but they had been washed. Who was I to reject them?

I took a pen and a pad of paper from the bedside table and went down to the pool an hour after my lunch.

The pool was on higher ground at the end of the garden. I passed a grass tennis court. The sun had baked it browner than green, but the surface looked flat and hard and ready for play.

The sun bore down on me, and so I was in the pool as

soon as I was ready. The water was warm, with the smell of a recently applied cleansing agent. There were lanes marked out the bottom of the pool, but I ignored them as first I swam on my front contemplating drowning as a means to end my guilt in Sandema. A couple of lengths later I turned over onto my back as the sun beat down its rays to burn me. Purgatory must be like this I thought.

In both exercises, I was unable to relax. The murders lay heavily on my mind. Yet the Russian hospitality was welcome. The police investigation in the north was more problematic. Surely some will have concluded I was no longer there at the Pioneer factory and with a dash or two they could actually betray me. Yet I knew I was in the safest place, as an embassy gave its own immunity. How long for I wondered. Then a plan began to formulate in my mind. A plan to escape.

I found a lounge chair in the shade of a bowing palm tree and I was dry in no time at all. I lifted up the pad of paper and began to write to Morag. I told her about the pool and the tennis court first and that I was staying in Accra. I was sure that would please her. Her six weeks elective might coincide with my time in Accra, but it was too soon to determine that. The events in Sandema did not feature in my letter. That was for a later chat or would it be a confrontation? I wrote at length of how I was missing her and counting down the days till she arrived in Accra.

Having written and addressed the letter I closed my eyes. The sun was soporific and the humidity of the south of the country made me feel drowsy. I was not expecting company.

'Is it Robert, the Scot?' a female voice asked in Russian.

I shaded my eyes and saw before me a red polka dotted bikini-clad woman of around forty years of age. I confirmed that I was indeed Robert. 'I am surprised you know who I am.'

'You are the spy who killed that man Desoto.'

There was no point denying it. This woman was probably the wife of a senior Russian diplomat.

'I can't deny that.' I replied as if it was a simple task.

'A messy task, but so necessary. We can't have defectors, can we?'

I made sure she saw me nod vigorously.

'And your duties in the embassy, can I ask?'

She laughed. 'My duty is to my husband Viktor, Second Secretary. My name is Darya.'

'So you know why I am here?'

'Of course. You are a fugitive. We will protect you. You are safe in this compound. It is Russia here.'

She lay down beside me on another lounger. My eyes closed at the brightness of the sun.

'You don't mind?'

I looked at her to understand her question as she undid the top of her bra and cast it aside. She lay on her back.

'I'm trying to get a suntan.'

'I see,' I said and got up to swim once more.

That night as we were about to sit down to a communal table, Vitaly drew me aside.

'I was not aware you had a girlfriend coming to Accra?'

'Ah, Morag. Yes, she is doing a six-week elective in tropical medicine at the Korle Bu teaching Hospital soon.'

'That's good. We hope to meet her sometime.'

'She will be very busy,' I said in haste, hoping to dissuade him from finding an espionage role for her.

'I imagine she will be very busy indeed, but surely she will want to see you—and here you are?'

I smiled at him. 'Yes, it could be a very welcome break for her. And me of course.'

'Of course.'

He introduced me at the table as the northern agent who has been doing fine work for the Soviet nation. I smiled and acknowledged his comment. He then told everyone that I was not only Scottish but a descendant of the much-loved poet, Robert Burns. This proved very popular. I had to ask how he knew.

'Utechin told us.'

'Ah yes, I remember us reciting a Burns poem one day.'

The meal was a combination of Russian and Ghanaian food. Avocado with chopped onion and vinegar for the starter, followed by a hot goulash with dumplings and a fresh bowl of fruit with a dollop of ice cream. Oh, how I enjoyed that meal.

The following day I was summonsed to Vitaly Karamanov's office, which was on the first floor looking over the front of the grounds.

'Take a seat. I have some sad news for you.'

Sad news for me? I could not think of anything other than that they were about to put me out, leaving me to fend for myself.

'Comrade Utechin died last night.'

There was a moment of silence as I absorbed the news.

'I knew he had been attending the Tamale General Hospital. Of course he drank—'

'You are right. He died of complications of cirrhosis in the liver.'

'He certainly showed the signs of jaundice and I sometimes I saw some blood in the washbasin. He had been coughing up blood. I was glad he was, at last, going to the hospital but obviously, it was much too late.'

'Yes, we knew of his drinking. He had been a good agent for so long—a soft job like running the Pioneer Peanut factory was his reward.'

Despite the despicable errand he gave me, he had been

jovial at times and I had warmed to him. I felt Peace would miss him most.

'Now I have two people in mind to take over. You can probably guess who.'

'I think Peace Assare or Sammy Nkansa would be good candidates.'

'Yes, but who would you chose?'

I took a moment to answer.

'I would go for Peace. She is a strong woman and I think, almost a decade after independence, it should be a Ghanaian. She is such a capable woman. Mr Nkansa? He is not universally popular. Peace is.'

'Then Peace it is. I'll go up and tell her,' Vitaly said in a matter of fact way.

'The funeral, I should really attend,' I suggested.

His smile disarmed me. 'There will be no funeral here. Comrade Utechin's body will be flown to Accra and we will fly it home. His funeral will be in Bologoye.'

'Is that between Moscow and Leningrad?'

With a slight nod of his head and a broad smile he said, 'you know your Russia well.'

Chapter 16
Supping in the Lion's Den

Morag would be with me in just under two weeks and then I'd have to admit that living in the Russian Embassy had been necessary and not just a holiday.

I was contemplating the day as I prepared for my morning walk around the grounds. Yes, I would stop to smell the sweet bougainvillea or the flamboyant white frangipane amid tropical ferns. Then the bell jangled in the wooden glass fronted bell cabinet in my room. There was no denying whose spring coil it was. It was the Ambassador's bell. He was summoning me to his office.

I knocked on his door and he shouted to me to come in. He was standing with his hand ready to shake mine.

'Are you enjoying our hospitality?' he asked by way of an opener.

'I can't fault it at all. I have made great use of the pool and the gardens. And of course, it has given me time to grow this beard,' I said caressing the growth over my chin.

He laughed. 'It suits you.'

'Thank you.'

'I hope Morag will like it,' the ambassador said.

He had obviously been aware of my letter. 'I hope I can serve again if I can, but I realise Ghana may be out of the question—following Sandema.'

He returned to his seat and from a silver case took out a cigarette. He offered one to me but I shook my head.

He exhaled. 'You must be wondering why I have brought you to my office.'

'Well, it did surprise me.'

'I have an assignment for you. On Saturday I have been invited to an evening of conversation and music at the British embassy. I want to take you with me.'

'Me! Why me? That would be like supping in the lion's den,' I said proudly to have been given such consideration by the ambassador.

He laughed as he blew out grey smoke. 'I'll take you as my aide de camp. Speak English with a Russian accent. Then we separate. You begin to mix. Find out what's happening. Listen to conversations. Adapt your story as you wish. You have a proven record as a liar. Keep it up.'

'I see, sort of being the eyes and ears and remembering any significant information.'

'Yes, and the not so interesting information too, of course.'

I was glad the ambassador thought I could be useful to him, but the British embassy was where I had been thinking of making my escape. I didn't want to risk being identified too closely with the Russian ambassador.

The days leading up to Saturday crawled by. Yet I had no time to write to Morag. My mind was still dominated by the murders. A minister's son brought up in the faith but still a murderer in the eyes of Sandema and elsewhere. It was uncomfortable beyond words can tell. My daily swims became twice daily though I kept my eyes from, by now, two Russian wives who sought over-all tans.

On Friday night, I was fitted with a dark blue suit with a short-sleeved blue shirt and tie. I tried on a selection of other clothes and they fitted fairly well. In the end, I decided to wear flannels and a bright and colourful Jeromi with intricate silver thread embroidered around the neckline.

On Saturday afternoon I had a siesta. It was four before I woke. My swim ended up being with two male embassy staff that seemed to know I was a spy. Everyone did. They asked a few questions. Our conversation, in Russian, was not stilted. They seemed to enjoy speaking to a westerner in their own language.

That evening at 6:45 p.m. it was as dark as fresh charcoal for burning. I set off with the ambassador on a journey of less than half-a-mile. The driver dropped us at the front door and drove away. There to greet us was a flunky who took our names and announced us as the Russian ambassador and his aide-de-camp.

We shook hands with the British ambassador and his charming wife and proceeded through the hallway to where there were open doors leading to the lawn. At the side of the staircase was a drinks table with bottles of local beer and glasses of champagne. Gin and tonics were ready to be served too with bottles of orange Fanta for the Tee-totals amongst us.

The ambassador went straight for the orange juice and after finishing one glass he drank another and then, with his hands free, began to circulate amongst the ambassadorial staff of many different nations.

I was pleased to see the Accra Police Band wore Jeromi shirts, as did many of the other guests. I circulated as much as possible away from the suited ambassadors looking for others more my age.

I encountered a group of British VSO teachers and nurses and had a lengthy chat with some of them. I was interested to hear that one young man was an economics teacher at the

Navrongo secondary school. I could not help but ask him about the poisoning cases.

'Oh yes, about a month ago. Well, the Kumasi police have returned home.'

'So they got the culprit?' I asked, feigning a general curiosity.

'No, I don't think so. They decided, as Sandema was so near the border of Upper Volta, that it made sense for the killer to cross over and make his escape from there. After all, they don't get our news in Upper Volta, and we certainly don't get theirs. So it looks like he's got off scot-free,' he laughed.

'Scot free, it's been a long time since I heard that expression,' I laughed, wondering if he knew more than he said.

I mixed with a few more VSOs and then found myself talking to some missionaries whose work covered the country. They all seemed more concerned with their local communities rather than bothering much with contact with other towns and they had no reason to mention the deaths in the north. Rather they quizzed me about the Russian Orthodox Church. It was not something I knew much about, so I hid behind a heavy Russian accent and struggled to find the words required in response. Yet I probably spent almost twenty minutes with them.

Then the police band began to play. As the night's entertainment for a British party, they played a selection of old English folk tunes—'Greensleeves', 'Blow the Wind Southerly' and 'The Keel Row' among them.

I approached the band as they came to the end of this collection of English songs. I said, 'Excuse me, why not play some Highlife?'

The request produced smiling faces and the conductor took his cue from them, and suddenly the guests started to move their hips in time with the music. I caught the eye of Comrade Leskov and he smiled at me. I was certainly integrating.

On Sunday morning the Ambassador sat with me at breakfast to hear my thoughts and impressions.

'So Robert, what did you think?'

'It was enjoyable, after all, I have not been out of the embassy for over two weeks—I heard that the extra police that was drafted to the north have been called off the murder enquiry in Sandema.'

'Really? Good.'

'An economics teacher from Navrongo told me they had come to the conclusion that the killer crossed over to French Upper Volta and made his escape from there.'

'Excellent. That means we can send you somewhere else, but not back north.'

I convincingly informed him I was ready to serve whenever and wherever that might be. Then my recollection of the previous night took hold of me.

'You know about Northern Ireland?' I asked.

'Yes, a divided community, not so?'

'Very much so. It's a religious thing too. Protestant workers in command and Roman Catholics trodden on. Things are getting out of hand.'

'I agree with your assessment, ripe for exploitation—but you didn't pick up on that last night, I'm sure.'

'But I did. One of the VSO teachers was a Catholic—from Belfast. He had flames coming out of his eyes he was so anti-British. He sees a civil war breaking out in mainland Britain. It's not far off, he told me.'

'I see.'

'Yes, and he predicts more bombings will be coming to England soon.'

'And where is this teacher working?'

'He's a science teacher at Ho in the Volta region.' I told him the man's name.

He took out his notepad and wrote the facts I had given him. 'You have done well Robert. Very well indeed.'

'Can you make use of this information?' I asked.

His smile seemed wider than the river Volga. 'Next week I have been recalled to Moscow. My superiors will take this on board. It sounds like something we could use to our advantage.'

Chapter 17
Morag arrives in Accra

My beard was itching. It had grown very full and it required a trim. I had that done a few days before Morag arrived. I looked in the mirror. I was still recognisable and I thought and I'd say my chin trim made me look more mature. But I would say that, wouldn't I?

At the poolside, there was much interest in the arrival of Morag. I tried to put them off on the grounds she would be very busy at the teaching hospital.

'Ah, Korle Bu. They opened the maternity wing last year. We helped to pay for it. Our ambassador and some of his staff attended the unveiling.' Darya laughed uncontrollably, as did her fellow sun worshipper.

I tried to interpret what was said. I drew a blank. When the laughter died down, she continued her story.

'Brigadier Amaney was the health minister. He drew back the curtain and announced that he was very pleased to be able to unveil the plague at the hospital.'

It made me laugh too, but the subject soon returned to Morag. They asked my intentions and I told them I had not seen her for such a long time. I'd have to see how we feel.

'So she is arriving this Saturday?'

'Yes, early. British Caledonian airways from Glasgow,' I

replied realising an early dip in the pool tomorrow was out of the question.

'Then I'll ask my husband to give you a driver.'

'That would be appreciated,' I replied with an eye squeezed, sun-avoiding smile at Darya.

'And he can bring you both back here for us to meet her,' she said looking at her friend.

I wanted to make the situation plain before they laid plans for her. 'You know she does not speak Russian?'

'But we speak English don't we,' she smiled with a glancing nod.

'I'd almost forgotten. Of course, your English is good. I've always spoken Russian to you.'

'Yes, and we love your accent.'

'My accent? How do you hear me,' I asked with interest.

'I'd say you speak with a Byelo accent.'

'A Byelo accent? My Russian teacher would be pleased to hear that.'

'You have a Russian tutor?'

'She began as a pen friend. I was studying modern languages at Glasgow University and she helped me a lot, especially in the Cyrillic writing.'

It was perhaps clear from her nod that Darya understood how I had been caught up in the spy net. She knew that Russian pen friends were used to enticing westerners. They always gave female pen friends to male contacts and vice versa.

And so the morning came. I was up at 5 a.m. and dressed, awaiting the driver. It was the First Secretary's car with Corps Diplomatique number plates. That meant we could park anywhere without restriction.

We arrived in good time. I entered the airport and found myself in a sea full of cleaners wielding mops and shop owners unlocking their doors.

I enquired about the flight. It was expected to be a few minutes late. There was time for a coffee while my driver, Samuel, sat with his Milo chocolate drink.

I drummed my fingers on the table while sipping the hot coffee. There was a churning inside me—I was sure our relationship was strong but I had to nip myself and accept that she was here to further her medical career, not sit and listen to all my woes.

I finished my coffee and went to dispose of the plastic cup. As I was dropping it from my hand I saw a speck of dirt on the lounge window. No, it was getting larger. Then I saw the lights, this was the plane. I stood mesmerised as it grew before my eyes.

The flight arrivals board confirmed the British Caledonian flight from Glasgow was about to land. I watched as the slender fuselage seemed to float past on the runway with its flaps at right angles to slow the brute down. It almost came to a stop, but then turned round to taxi into gate 4.

I watched as the passengers got off the plane in an orderly line, heading for the customs. I saw Morag. She looked pale, unsurprisingly. She was not looking my way. The sun would have been in her eyes. My heart seemed to want to jump out of me. My pulse rate was up. Was that because I had so much to tell her; so much to explain? Would she believe me and, either way, could I repair the damage? My mind was in a fankle, like a rugby scrum.

I stood awaiting her to appear from the customs' room. First out were three nuns in their light grey habits. They seemed like a gang of excited school children. A Christian father welcomed them and amid excited chatter, they left, inevitably heading off to some mission station. A pram with a child appeared and a couple guiding it with a case-laden trolley. Seven, presumably Ghanaians, appeared showing their Harrods's attire from the city store in London—and then there she was.

I opened my arms wide. She saw me and her mouth opened in excitement. Then she stroked her chin. I did the same and knew the beard was not an instant put-me-off.

She dropped her bags as I approached. I ran to her and we lingered in a satisfying hug. I squeezed her as she did me and I felt my life was changing back to normal once more. My lips settled on her cheek. She moved her head away and returned to kiss me full on the lips.

'I've missed you like…like the last bus to Govan,' I said.

She laughed at my nonsense. 'I've missed you and dreamt of you most nights.'

'And the other nights?' I asked with a grin.

'Studies, seminars and practicals. Then more dreams of you.'

The scent of something appealing was behind her ears. Carbolic soap was all I had at the embassy, but at least my morning shower made me feel fresh.

'Your beard…it suits you. It's not too hot for one in the tropics is it?' she asked as we separated, and she took a step back to view the change.

'It is not a permanent fixture,' I said without thinking. 'I'd love to tell you I grew it for you. But it's a long story.'

'Don't shave for me. I think I like it. It suits you.'

Her words were very welcome. No further explanation was required, there and then. We came forward once more and in those loving moments, we talked in syncopation about missing each other, looking forward to the next six weeks.

'Our car is waiting outside. When have you to report to the hospital?' I asked hastily.

'By this evening, so we can spend half of today together, yes?'

'Then let me show you where in Accra I'll be for the next few weeks.'

She pondered what I had said. 'The Pioneer Peanuts factory will come to a halt without you, surely?'

All I could do was smile. Too much information as she faced a new medical challenge was not what she needed. I'd have to drip feed my story like intravenous fluids, at the right time.

Morag did not look often at me as she tried to soak up the smells and sights of a new country, on a new continent. The crickets gave uninterrupted applause to her ears as we got into the back seat of the car.

As we drove off, I pointed out to her the wayside trader's goods and explained that the car swerved so much to avoid potholes. She was thrilled to see the vibrant cloth the women wore and I told her that the women were the economic gurus of the market and the knots they made in their waistbands contained many cedi notes. The women usually earned more than their husbands, I added. She noticed that many of the men offered car maintenance services and tailoring facilities which seemed to occupy every third kiosk. Then the car entered the more affluent embassy residential district.

Chapter 18
Morag and Robert at the Pool

As the car swept into and up the Embassy drive, Morag let out a gasp. 'You are living here—in the Russian embassy?'

'Yes, for the time being, to be near you. Wasn't that kind of them?'

'Kind of whom, Robert?'

My response needed more time, so I simply raised my finger to my lips. She gave me a quizzical look taking my silent instruction to heart.

Vitaly Karmanov stood at the entrance to meet Morag.

'Delighted to meet you, doctor,' he said shaking her unsteady hand.

'I should say, First Secretary, that Morag is not quite a doctor yet, but her opportunity to experience tropical medicine here will take her further down that road.'

'I'm very pleased to meet you and grateful that you are able to host Robert while I am here,' she said, giving a generous smile.

'Who am I to thwart true love?' Vitaly said, with a smile as wide as an eagle's wingspan. 'Take her bags to the reception Samuel, and Robert go to the conservatory with your fiancée for a refreshing drink—I am sure Morag will appreciate that after such a long flight.'

Morag glanced at me on hearing the word fiancée. I

opened my hand and waved her through the reception area to the conservatory, where several fans whirled away helping to keep things tolerably cool.

'This is so palatial. Not what I expected.'

'Nor I. I'll tell you about it by the pool.'

'There's a pool?'

'Out the back. You'll love it,' I said, seeing a servant arrive with our drinks. I stood up. The servant offered us two fresh orange ice-filled glasses from the tray. I took them both and passed one to Morag.

'May I join you?' asked Vitaly, entering the spacious room.

'Please do,' I said.

He sat opposite us.

'I'm delighted that you were able to bring Robert down from Tamale,' Morag said.

'You are at Korle Bu for six weeks, not so?' Vitaly said.

'Yes.'

'Then Robert will be here for the duration of your stay in Accra. He won't be returning to Tamale.'

'He won't be returning to Tamale? Not even after I leave?'

Vitaly shook his head. 'We are indigenising the factory. Letting the locals take over. They are ready for that. Robert did a fine job bringing them on. As I say, it's time for them to take over.'

Morag sipped her orange juice, clinking her ice cubes as she did. 'So, if Robert is not going back to Tamale, have you decided on another place, or will he be coming home?'

I saw the importance of her question. It made me uncomfortable, yet I needed to know what was on Vitaly's mind.

'Well, that's a good question. I guess there are a few options. We could find him a job elsewhere, outside Ghana perhaps—we could offer you both a post if you wish? We could send him back to Europe too.'

Morag smiled. 'You mean back to Scotland?'

Vitaly sipped his drink then placed the glass purposefully down on his coaster. 'Europe is a big continent. Scotland is not out of the question.'

'Vitaly, Morag has to be at the hospital later today. Perhaps there's time to go to the pool soon?'

'Yes, excellent idea and be back for lunch at 1 p.m.' he said as he coaxed the last few orange bits out of his glass. Then he left the conservatory.

Each time Morag tried to ask a sensitive question, I placed my finger to my lips then I tapped my ear. She gleaned it was not always safe to talk openly.

At the pool, seeing it was only mid-morning, I lay out two sun loungers opposite where my afternoon position usually was. This was near a garden plot of herbs. I looked around. I lowered my voice as Morag laid her towel over her white shins.

'Always suspect there is a recording device around.'

'I can speak Glaswegian if you wish?' she joked.

'I think we are safe here. Not many swims in the morning. If there's a microphone around, I suspect it's on the other side of the pool. There's not much cover for a mike around the sun loungers here.'

'Well, wherever it is, I need some answers, Robert. What the hell is going on? You've lost your job and they bend over backwards for you here in Accra, just because I've arrived. It doesn't make sense. Their generosity is outstanding. Why?'

'You are right. It doesn't make sense. I've been a fool. I'm caught up in something. There's much to tell you but not here. Come on let's get into the pool.'

'Last one in is a sissy,' she said.

I took a leap into the water after her. When I surfaced, I saw Vitaly at the window.

Chapter 19
Korle Bu Teaching Hospital

Korle Bu hospital had a brightly shining entrance. Palm trees with their sprayed branches seem to wave Morag a welcome. The sea was not far away and the smell of decaying seaweed gave our nostrils a twinge.

I insisted on carrying Morag's baggage, thus depriving several impoverished helpers. I suppose I did not wish to share Morag with anyone.

At the reception, Morag showed her letter of appointment and the receptionist lifted the telephone.

As she waited for a reply, she held her hand over the mouthpiece. 'Take a seat over there for a moment, please.'

We sat down and Morag looked around. 'It's a very modern hospital.'

'It certainly is. I hope your placement goes well for you.'

'Me too. Can we talk freely now?'

'Looks like Korle Bu will be our free-to-talk place from now on.'

'So, let's get it right from the very start. What is going on? You have not been totally open with me in your letters.'

'I know. I will give you all the facts. I need to offload a lot. I think I already told you, it began on holiday, on Jura.'

That was all I could say. A doctor was approaching with a welcoming smile.

'I'm Dr Amma Swaniker. I am delighted to meet you,' she said to Morag. 'So you are from Scotland, Glasgow University. I did my postgraduate medicine at Edinburgh University.'

'Then you know Scotland well,' Morag said.

'I visited many parts. It's a beautiful country. Now, is this—your husband?'

'No, Robert is not my husband.'

'Ah, I see. Well, we don't allow men coming to the unmarried doctors' rooms.'

I could see Morag's shoulders drop. She was not happy with what she had just been told, especially as she was anxious to learn more about her boyfriend. 'No he's not my husband. He's my fiancé,' she replied with feeling.

A shudder went through my body. Her statement sounded so good. But I suspected she only said it so she could learn more of my situation while out of the earshot of the Russian embassy.

'I see, then that's quite different. You didn't inform us of your engagement.'

'I do apologise. We have not been engaged very long,' Morag said, clearly uncomfortable with lying. I sympathised with her.

'Let me take you over to the doctor's quarters.' She talked as we walked. 'You'll find A&E behind reception. That is where you report—tomorrow at 8 a.m.' She turned to me. I detected her question.

'Robert Harvie,' I said.

'Mr Harvie, you have accommodation in Accra?'

'Yes, on the outskirts of the city.'

'I see,' she said and to further satisfy her curiosity she enquired, 'what line of work you are engaged in, may I ask.'

'It's diplomatic work.'

'Ah, of course. The residential compounds near the airport.'

'Yes, that's right.'

'You have a fine group of diplomatic staff at the British embassy.'

'You know us?' I asked, with more than a degree of concern about my lies.

'Not for a while. I have not been back to Scotland for several years now. My visa has certainly lapsed. The staff will have changed by now anyway, I am sure.'

'Yes, our tours are not that long,' I said.

'Then I think we should give you both a double room rather than the one I had planned. It has a double bed.'

I could have kissed this doctor at that moment. But she had a further word of caution.

'There is a curfew of course, even for those who are engaged. It is at 10 p.m.' She unlocked the door. The room was sun-drenched, with a view over the sea.

'What a beautiful room,' said a delighted Morag.

'There is an information pack on the dressing table. Meals are in the doctors' dining room, but the kitchen is always open if you require food out of hours. You, Mr Harvie can eat with Morag when you are here.

'Well, I'll leave you to unpack. Give me a ring if you have any questions. There's bound to be a few in a new hospital, so far from home.'

'You have made us feel so welcome. I am sure my placement will go well,' said Morag, smiling.

'Let me give you an Akan Twi proverb. *Kakra, kakra Akawkaw benum nsu*. It literally means; slowly, slowly the hen drinks water. You can just imagine that, can't you? It means you are new with much to learn in our culture. So, do it bit by bit, just as the hen drinks water. Enjoy your afternoon.'

With that proverb still in our minds she left and we stood together silent for a moment.

'Engaged? When did that happen?' I asked. We laughed and then we cuddled. 'It sounded good to me.'

'Well maybe one day,' she said.

I felt good to hear that. We sauntered over to the window and looked out into the Gulf of Guinea.

'You are as pretty as ever, I could not have found a better girl. I really love you,' I said.

There was a moment's pause.

'I love you too Robert. But we've got to get you out of this mess you are in. Whatever it is. So, start from the beginning again. Tell me after you were on holiday on Jura…start there once more.'

Chapter 20
Labadi Beach Club

When I returned that night to my embassy room, I lay down on the bed, mesmerised by the revolving wings of the ceiling fan above me.

Morag had learned of my route to Ghana, and finally, I had explained the murders I could still be charged with. It shocked her of course yet she saw I was not the instigator of death. Her condolences were so reassuring for me. My secrets were off my mind, the way was clear for me. How clear it was for Morag I was yet to discover.

The next morning, Vitaly joined me at breakfast. He pulled up a chair.

'Is Morag well?'

'Yes, she'll be starting her first day by now.'

'A pretty girl.'

'Yes, that's true,' I said taking a bite of buttered toast.

'Known her long?' he enquired.

I chewed a little more then held a cup of tea between both hands. 'Yes, we met not long after we became students at Glasgow University.'

'That's a few years ago now, isn't it?'

I smiled at him. 'Guess so.'

'If an engagement party was on the cards, we'd just love to host it here.'

'Well I can't guarantee anything—but it's on my mind, I assure you.'

Vitaly rose from the table and slapped my back as he was leaving. 'Come up to my room, I have something for you.'

My eyes followed him out of the dining room. What could he possibly have for me? I finished my tea and returned to my room to brush my teeth. The brush sped hurriedly over my teeth; up and down, up and down, and as I spat out into the basin, I wondered if he had found something to occupy my duration in Accra. A quick comb of the hair and beard and I was on my way to his door. I knocked and waited.

'Come in Robert,' he said in Russian, the language in which we spoke at the embassy on every occasion.

I saw on his table that he had a racquet, a squash racquet, laid across two files.

'You play squash?'

'I played a few games at university. Prefer badminton actually,' I said relieved that there appeared to be no sinister intentions on his mind.

'I don't have a badminton racquet. But I do know a squash court.'

'This is very kind of you. I think Morag could play too.'

He shook his head. 'No, Robert, this is work. I want you to go every Wednesday night to the Labadi Beach Sports Club. It's where the expat community gather on a Wednesday night. It has a pool and a tennis court too, but they seem short of squash players. It's after the game that you earn your stay. That's when they socialise over a couple of beers. You understand?'

'Yes, so far,' for I knew there was more on his mind.

'You will take note of anything interesting they might say. Get their names, find out where they work, who their contacts are.'

'Will I use my own name?'

'No, I have cover for you. You are Ewan Shankland. You work as an accountant for the Ghanaian owned African Trading Company in Usshertown in Accra. Go along this afternoon and join the club. They are likely to ask which activities you are interested in. Say squash, and perhaps swimming. Then you will be invited to join. Tell them Wednesday nights suit you. Take it from there. Mind you no Russian. You are British of course, this time. Go over there on Tuesday to get your membership card and see the lie of the land. Any questions?'

'No, I'll see what I can find out.'

'You are a Godsend Robert, I mean Ewan,' he said, and I got up to leave with my racquet.

At 5 p.m. on Tuesday afternoon I arrived at the Labadi club. The staff was very obliging. I was met by cheerful smiles and in no time at all, I had a member's card in my hand and had paid 10 cedis for my first three months. I asked if many played squash and to what standard.

'Some are very good and some are just beginners,' I was told. That was a good omen. I had a look around the clubhouse seeing names on the tennis championship board going back to the turn of the century. Only the years 1939-45 had no winners. There were several Macs and Jones and an array of other British names too. It was doubtful if any of them still frequented the club yet their presence seemed to linger in the old oak barstools.

'Sir, can I get you a drink?'

'Ah yes, a good idea. Have you a Tata beer?'

'Sorry no Tata. We have Guilder or Club, sir.'

'Then a pint of Guilder please.'

'Where will you be sitting?'

I looked around. There was a table near the tennis court where a ladies' foursome was underway.

'Over there,' I pointed.'

I was more than halfway through my glass when their game finished. They left the court and simply had to pass by my table.

'Well played, ladies,' I said.

'Thank you,' the tallest one said.

'Are you a visitor?' asked another.

'No longer. I just joined,' I said twisting my membership card between two fingers like a stage magician.

'Then you can join us for tennis.'

'Actually, squash is my preferred game. I gather we can play on Wednesday evenings.'

'Yes, that's right. Roger, my husband plays then. You'll meet him tomorrow tonight.'

I smiled at her.' And how will I recognise your handsome husband?'

All four ladies laughed like school children.

'Roger is six feet five, need I say more?'

My eyebrows raised an inch. 'Six foot five, then it looks like he'll cover the court better than anyone. I'm sure to be the loser.'

'I warn you they seem to spend more time drinking than playing squash,' Roger's wife guffawed.

'It's a challenging game,' I found myself saying.

'Yes. So you are visiting Accra, or do you work here?' the red-haired tennis player asked.

'I've only been in Accra for three weeks. I work at the African Trading Company at Usshertown. I am their accountant.'

'Oh, I must get you to do my tax return,' laughed the smallest tennis player. I'm sorry—I did not catch your name.'

'Ewan Shankland.'

'Shankland, Shankland. It's a Scottish name isn't it?'

'Yes, lowland Scot.'

'Are you related to a Bill Shankland, by any chance, a college lecturer in Dumfries?'

'Er…no, not our branch of the family,' I said, hoping that would end her enquiry.

'So not married yet, I see,' said Roger's wife staring at my left hand.

'No, but my fiancée is studying at Korle Bu Teaching Hospital.'

'Three weeks? My, that way quick, Romeo,' she said and they all laughed.

'I've been with her for some time. She's also from Glasgow,' I said to clarify the situation.

That night I made my way by tro-tro lorry to the hospital. I went straight up to Morag's room and knocked. There was no reply. I looked at my watch it was 8 p.m. I returned to reception and asked when Morag would be off duty. I was told she would end her shift at 10 p.m.

I sat down, hoping she might pass by. I wrote a note to tell her I could not visit on Wednesday nights because I would be playing squash at Labadi. As there was still no sight of her, I approached the reception desk and asked the lady on duty to give my note to Morag.

'I'll put it in her pigeon-hole for you sir,' she replied and did so before my eyes.

'I am much obliged,' I said.

I decided to walk back home, passing many food vendors selling—roasted groundnuts, fried kelewele plantain slices and leaves of sour banku dough. The crickets clicked unseen and a few stray dogs lingered, hoping to be thrown a morsel of something edible.

The following day was Wednesday. It dragged as I waited to start another mission. I hoped my last. I saw this task as something of a social outlet—not as dangerous as the tin of chocolates. But I thought it would take some time to get to know who was who. I went to the club dressed in white shorts and a blue top, reinforcing my status as a Scot, perhaps. I had borrowed plimsolls from a games box in the embassy's gazebo. Vitaly approved my rigout.

When I arrived, with my squash racquet well to the fore, I was met by Morgan, who took me through to the court. He was clearly Welsh—he said he worked for Barclay's bank. His shirt sported Barclay's Bank logo.

'Hi, pleased to meet you, Ewan. Played much then?'

'Not for years. Probably not even up-to-date with the rules,' I said with a glum face.

'Sounds like you are my standard. When these two come off, we can play.'

'They look good,' I observed. 'Who are they?'

'Kevin is from Larne. He's in the pale blue top. Willy Salmond is from Edinburgh, he's a vicar at the Ridge Church in town.'

'So, no foul language on court.' I joked—I recalled my father identifying this Willy Salmond for me before I left Glasgow. At last, I would be able to say we had met.

'Don't you believe it Ewan, Willy swears like a trooper if he misses an easy shot. He leaves his collar behind on a Wednesday night.'

'And Kevin? What does he do out here?'

'Kevin is a vet at the university.'

'I see. Oh, and I heard there was some player who was six-foot plus.'

'You mean Roger?'

'Yes, that's his name.'

'You know him?'

'I met his wife when I came out to get my membership card yesterday afternoon.'

'She'd be playing tennis,' he said.

I nodded my agreement.

'So, membership? Not a passing visitor. You must be working around here then?'

'Yes, I'm the accountant at the African Trading Company,' I lied confidently.

'That's a safe job.'

My eyes tightened. 'What do you mean?'

'A European accountant avoids the risk of embezzlement. No local family dashes. Not so?'

'Dashes?' I enquired.

'Yes, tips.'

'Oh, I see now yes, I've heard the word loads of times. So that's what it means.'

'You must come to our banking dos. Our accountants and managers, along with their wives, meet once a month. Bring your wife too.'

'I'd like to but I don't have a wife, just a girlfriend.'

'A Ghanaian girl?' he asked raising his voice slightly.

'No Morag is a Scot too. She's at Korle Bu teaching hospital.'

'Bring her along. Give me your telephone number at the bar after we play. Hey… look. They are coming off, our turn.'

We played the best of three. At first, I was slow, but I eventually got up to speed. My eye focussed and I began to win some shots. That boosted my confidence, especially as I saw onlookers above me, assessing my standard. I lost the first game 8-11. However, I rallied well and took the second game 11-9, and won the decider 13-11.

There was hardly a moment lost when Roger entered the court. He tapped my shoulder as I left, to acknowledge me, or was it my performance? I watched him play and felt we were all of a similar standard which was reassuring.

'Morgan, so what does Roger do?'

'Rodger is a useful guy. He works for the Black Star Line—the shipping company. Gets things cleared from customs as quick as you like. A very useful man.'

I played twice against Roger, but he beat me at both games. I put it down to his size and reach. Perhaps I was a bad loser. Willy and Kevin had the final game and then we sat in the open as the waiter took our orders.

Crickets crowded the ground lamps and the hissing of a garden hose kept the lawn green. My Guilder arrived—all had a beer except Willy, whose orange juice matched Kevin's top.

Morgan went into his sports bag and produced a phial of pills. He laid them out and everyone took one. I bent forward to see what they were.

'Salt tablets. You lose so much sweat playing you need to replace the salt. This does the trick. We always take one. It's not an illicit drug,' Kevin said with a sort of a snigger and the others laughed as they saw me relax.

We were halfway through our beers when Morgan raised the hairs on the back of my neck. 'These murders up in Sandema, they haven't got him yet have they?'

'A white man in the North? I bet he's gone a long time ago. I can't see how he could hide up there for any length of time,' said Willy.

'They should call out the Met to help them,' suggested Kevin.

It was time for me to muddy the waters. 'I've a hunch, he was probably French and crossed over back into French West Africa pretty quick.'

'Then why did he come to Ghana in the first place, to do his dirty work then?' asked Willy.

We sat silently for a full thirty seconds thinking about Willy's point and of any other interpretation.

'So Ewan, what brought you out to Ghana?'

I was relieved the subject had changed. However, it was time to lie once more. 'I always enjoyed geography at school. The dark continent, the white man's grave, Mungo Park's allure for the continent, not to mention an uncle who fought in the Ashanti Wars. It all galvanised me to apply to work in Ghana. And here I am.'

'When did you arrive in Accra?' asked Willy. 'I've not seen you around.'

'I've been in the city for three weeks now.'

'You are a quick worker, Ewan. He's got a girlfriend in Accra already,' said Morgan, laughing while wiping his handkerchief over his sweaty brow.

'Three weeks, that's fast work Ewan,' joked Kevin.

'Well I had one other reason for coming here specifically. My girlfriend is doing medicine at Glasgow. She wanted to do some tropical work and got a place at the Korle Bu Teaching Hospital—and so I wanted a three-month placement and got six instead at the African Trading Company.'

'Does she play squash?' asked Kevin.

'You know, I've never asked her.'

Chapter 21
Home truths

I asked to see Vitaly urgently the following morning.

'It was like being in a lion's den,' I began. 'I was asked for my telephone number but got out of that one for the time being. I forgot to give it. They know I'm supposed to work for the African Trading Company. What happens if one of them phones the company this morning?' I said with my fists clenched.

'Relax, Robert. We can prepare a business card for you for next week.'

'But if they phone the trading company this morning?'

'Relax I said. If they phone the African Trading Company this morning, Yaa will direct the call here.'

I thought for a moment. Was Yaa a servant of the Russian state?

'We finance the African Trading Company. Just like the Groundnut factory. Of course—we do not speak about it. Rest assured if anyone calls to speak to you, Yaa will put the call through to me.'

I sat back in relief for a moment, but only briefly. 'The Welshman works for Barclay's bank. They have monthly soirées—the accountants and the bankers and their wives. I have been invited to attend the next one with Morag. You approve?'

'Approve? Of course. There might be some information you could find in that scenario.'

That night I returned to see Morag. I found her in the staff dining room, where she was slicing through some fresh pineapple. She put her fork down and pulled out a seat for me.

'Finished work for the day?' I asked.

'Yes, but keep your affections till later. The eyes of many are watching us.'

'You sound like a spy,' I laughed.

'No laughing matter, this spying of yours. It does worry me.'

'Well, the latest is that I am playing squash on a Wednesday night.'

'Yes, I got your note. That's good. Out of the embassy and meeting normal people, at last.'

'I'm meant to listen out for something valuable or perhaps just of interest, but I do enjoy their company.'

'You mean it wasn't you who decided on playing squash, it was the Russians?'

'Yes, but they only set the ground rules. I play their game and only give them harmless information.'

'Let's go to my room to talk,' she said.

As she unlocked the door I told her we were invited to the next banker's soiree.

'Us?' she enquired.

'Yes, us, that's you Morag Sutherland and me— Ewan Shankland.'

'Ewan Shankland? For God's sake, whatever next?'

'It's my final job for them. I'm Ewan Shankland, an accountant at the African Trading Company here in Accra. That's my cover.'

She stood still before me. I was unsure of how she would respond. What I had said might have ended our relationship and if it did, I had only myself to blame. But I saw a glint of understanding in her eyes.

'Oh Robert, darling. You are a puzzle at times. Yet I see how you are still trapped.'

She came close and put her arms around my waist.

'We are on the homeward leg. I have devised an escape plan but can only put it into practice when you leave to return home. I've thought it through and know I can pull it off. But don't ask me about it.'

She kissed me. I kissed her and we sat on the bed as a tear fell from my eye. It caused her tears to fall too.

'Robert, I have to start work tomorrow at 6 a.m. That means up at 5 a.m. I'm getting tired.'

I could see she was tired from being on her feet all day, and tired of my service to the Russians.

'Okay, I'd better be on my way. It's been a difficult week.'

I stood up and faced Morag. She stood too. I was expecting a good-night kiss. Instead, she said, 'Will you stay with me here tonight?'

And I did.

When I woke the following morning I was alone. Morag was already at work on a ward. I took a shower and dressed. Then I saw a paper on her side of the bed. It was more than a note—a billet-doux. It read:

I did not wake you as my eyes dwelt on your sleeping body this early morning. I thought, but could not say, I'd like to wake up each day with you. Perhaps that gives you an indication of the way I feel for you.

Take care in all you do. Be safe. I trust you.

Love Morag xxx

I folded the note and placed it in my linen jacket pocket. I left the hospital that morning with my head in the clouds. I only hoped my departure was discreet. I had broken the hospital rules.

I did not head straight to my room in the embassy but deviated through Makola market square, where a hive of colourful activity unfolded before my eyes. Pyramids of tomatoes and borders of onions lined the aged wooden tables. An array of traditional Kente cloths contrasted with the rich blue sky. The stench of drying fish balanced on the heads of the market women caught my nose and made me hold my breath.

I continued past endless begging —'please mister, buy some…' of…this or that. However I was on a specific mission and I found the shop I had in mind at the far end of the market, on Kojo Thompson Road.

I got back to the embassy around mid-day and was greeted by Ambassador Leskov.

'A fruitful excursion, Robert?' he asked, his manner paternal.

I gave a disarming smile. 'The sports club is likely to throw up some interesting information,' I said hoping to satisfy him. But his mind was elsewhere.

He placed his arm on my shoulder and moved me along the path bordering the front lawn.

'Your doctor friend—is she just an acquaintance in Accra, a friendly white face, or something much more?'

'I'd say much more. I don't deny I am very much in love.'

'I see.'

We continued to walk and I realised he might have plans for both of us. My inkling gained credence with his next words.

'Would you, the two of you, be willing to take on a position somewhere else? I have a place in mind.'

I felt pins and needles prickling me and sweat break out on my forehead,

'You realise she is still a student? She has to complete her final year back in Glasgow.'

'Ah, of course. But if we found a hospital or clinic for her—to work in Bolivia.'

'Bolivia! Why there? What would I do?'

'You speak Spanish, not so?'

'Er…yes.'

'Then Bolivia because Hugo Banzer is in power. The scourge of the left. He has imprisoned and had tortured many left-wing dissenters. He needs to be toppled.'

'So where does his power lie?'

'With America, of course.'

That night I returned to the hospital. I simply had to tell Morag about the Ambassador's plans for us, but stressed it was our future what mattered to me. She was in total agreement.

'So what do you intend to do?' she asked.

'It looks like I'll be able to come home with you and—well, you complete your studies and then we find work and make ourselves unavailable to the Russians.'

'Do you think it will be as easy as that?'

I knew there was no certainty in dealing with the Russians, but so far I had coped quite well. I had reason to believe I could pull it off. 'I think we can do it, and I'm keeping you out of their grasp. They have no reason to recruit you.'

She hugged me and we kissed.

'Morag, I've reached that magical moment. Have you?'

She looked at me quizzically. I took a pace backwards and

placed my hand in my back pocket. As I brought out the silver-lined box, I knelt before her.

'Morag darling, I love you so much. Will you be my wife?'

I could have sworn almost ten silent seconds elapsed, but I saw her smile grow wider by each moment.

'Yes, of course, Robert, of course I'll marry you.'

She took the engagement ring from its box and placed it on her marriage finger. 'It fits.'

Then we kissed again.

'We are so alone. No family to join in our happiness.'

'You have a phone here. Can you ring your parents?'

It was not the clearest of lines and the synchronisation of voices left much to be desired. I managed to speak to her parents briefly and expressed my love for their daughter while apologising for not requesting her hand in marriage in person. Her father wondered if the marriage would be in Ghana or Scotland. I replied it would be in Motherwell in just over a year after Morag qualified.

After Morag replaced the telephone in its carriage, we kissed once more.

'You can stay the night again. I'd like that.'

'Darling, so would I.'

Chapter 22
An Engagement Honour

There was general excitement around the embassy when they learned of my engagement. The female staff asked if there would be an engagement party and I could not give an answer, but by the time Vitaly had heard the news, party planning was well underway.

I telephoned Morag to let her know that on Saturday, as long as she was not working, there would be an engagement party at the embassy. Excited, she let me know that was in order, and she said she would have to look out for a suitable dress.

I was out of my depth at this point. In fact, I pinched myself. It was Wednesday and I hoped to get a dribble of intelligence to please my handlers that evening.

I mentioned the dress issue to one of the embassy wives and she was quick to suggest taking a few dresses over to Morag to see if they would fit. I thought that a good idea and left a message for Morag that there would be a dress drop at her room that evening.

I looked at my watch. It was time to get to the Labadi sports club.

Coming off the court sweating like Derby winners, we all took our salt tablets and started our pints of Guilder beer.

We were on our second and final beers when the conversation took an interesting turn.

'Two of my staff got new cars this week—from the British embassy,' Morgan said.

'That's funny. My secretary got one from them too,' said vet Kevin.

'I hear that they sell them off before returning home at the end of their tour,' said Morgan raising his eyebrows.

'There should be plenty of offers for the ambassador's Bentley,' I suggested and some laughter followed.

'No,' said Morgan. 'It's not at that level, Ewan. It's the number fours to sevens that are selling them. They bring out new cars, and after two years get them polished up and sell them on, making a bomb of a profit. The ambassador seems to turn a blind eye to it all. Yet he might have no knowledge of what's happening.'

My ears were straining to get all the details of how it worked. I felt I had an issue at last.

Willy shook his head. 'Greed and exploitation, that's what it is. Need to get some of the embassy staff onto my pews.' A nervous laugh came from the gathered agnostics.

'Anyway, they're poorly paid at that level. Guess they see it as a perk,' said a dreamy-eyed Roger. 'I see the cars coming in with their CD stickers at the port. Not so many go out.'

On Thursday morning I described the scenario to Vitaly. He was extremely interested. He told me it would put some bargaining power in their hands the next time they met the British delegation.

'Bargaining power is that not blackmail?'

'Call it what you want Robert, it's good intelligence, well done.'

I accepted his praise and felt I had not damaged the

Crown too much. At least if my plan went well I could explain it better to the British High Commissioner.

That night I was back at the hospital. Morag confirmed that two ladies had arrived with a collection of dresses the evening before. 'Darling you clearly did not indicate what size I was.'

'So none fitted?'

'One was so big it could have fitted two Russian grandmothers.'

I sat down on the edge of the bed. 'Cut to the chase, did you get one to fit?'

'Stay there,' she demanded. She went into the bathroom and changed. She came out in shining patent black shoes, a necklace and a bright red dress. On her left hand was the glint of the engagement ring sitting proudly in place.

'You look gorgeous. I wish I had my camera.'

'The dress is not mine to keep but it certainly seems to suit my hair.'

'You will steal the show,' I said with sincerity.

'I should, shouldn't I? After all it's our engagement party.'

She turned around in front of the mirror. She flicked her hair back. She seemed very satisfied with her dress.

'Robert, can you undo the zip at the back?'

I had found a way to be useful.

Later that night we made tentative arrangements for our wedding. My father was the obvious choice of a participating clergyman. And there could be a reception at the Bute halls at the university. Or perhaps dad could partake at her parent's church, St Andrew's, in Motherwell. We could not decide. A date had to be arranged but that did not worry us. We'd wait till nearer Morag's graduation. But time was moving on. There were only twenty-one days of Morag's placement at the Korle Bu teaching hospital left.

The engagement party was wonderful. The Accra City Brass Band played highlife music in the well-lit garden and there were guests from the Romanian, Polish, Czech, Cuban and Chinese embassies. They had been told of the engagement party and so a collection of presents appeared from them. A silk dress for Morag and a silk tie for me from China; an invitation to stay at the Bucharest Ramada Parc hotel for a week for two from Romania. Then came the speeches. The Russian Ambassador was the first to speak.

'Comrades, it is a pleasure to have the services of Robert Harvie. A fluent Russian speaker from Scotland who has served the red flag with dignity and honour.'

I caught Morag's eye as this tribute progressed amid some applause. She seemed mesmerised by the pomposity on show.

'And so it gives me pleasure in awarding Comrade Harvie with the Lenin Medal for outstanding service rendered to the State. Robert, step forward please.'

I did as I was told and stood before Ambassador Misha Leskov. He shook my hand amid more applause then turned me round to fasten the medal with a red and yellow edged ribbon around my neck.

'And a gift for his fiancée. Something which will be of no interest to your Robert. 'Morag, a box of Chocolate Gingerbread from Tula.' The Russians' present brought vigorous clapping, knowing this was indeed a special chocolate treat.

Then the Polish Ambassador stepped forward—Bogna Poczekaj-Ryszczuk. She was dressed in a mint-green two-piece suit of some light material, suitable for the climate. Her face was oval and her fair hair lay straight. She was a career woman, probably heading for a more significant posting before too long.

'It is with great pleasure we learned of this romance, and it is not only a unique occasion but a rather rare one too, in diplomatic services. You are both young, but you have achieved much in your short lives. Morag we need women doctors and I know wherever you may serve in the future you will be able to support your husband and fulfil a valuable role yourself. We would also wish to be associated with Comrade Robert's work and so I now ask you to come forward to receive the Bronze Polish Cross of Merit for your exemplary duty to communism.'

I was overwhelmed with these unsuspected honours, though all I really wanted was to get back to Scotland, marry Morag and end this bizarre stage of my life. Yet I did not show this in my heart-felt responses to their generosity.

Food was laid out on a side table and everyone had a plate in one hand and a glass of wine perched nearby on the table or on one of the bookcases which lined the room. We tried to stay together as much as possible. Morag's ring shone a clear bright light whenever it caught the shining candelabra. All the ladies wanted to see and touch it. Those with more than a spattering of English spoke to Morag, while I attracted the Russian speakers.

Ambassador Leskov struck a coin on a glass. He immediately got our attention.

'Forgive me. There is just one more announcement to make. How could I have forgotten?' The guests stared at each other, wondering what was on his mind.

'I wish to inform you that Robert Harvie has been promoted and will forthwith be located in Bolivia. His fiancée will join him after they are married in Scotland.'

Thunderous applause resounded for some time. After all, the Russian ambassador had found an excellent agent and was ready to exploit him further.

The brass band had had their break and they struck up some strangely familiar Scottish airs. I suspected some of the band had been schooled at Mons, or at Sandhurst and had memories of celebrating Burn's Night in the barracks.

We danced on the lawn in each other's arms and Morag whispered in my ear. 'I don't like their plans for you Robert.'

I buried my face in her hair as eyes turned discreetly away from the loving couple. 'Nor do I, but my plan is being thought through.'

Chapter 23
Planning Political Asylum

My information about the British embassy staff car scam had gone down well. So, I was encouraged to get to the Labadi beach club more often and mix freely, which I did. I had to be seen keeping up my espionage to my host's satisfaction. In fact, I was now at the club four days a week. It was a time of freedom. I knew there were no listening devices there, and it was an excellent place to meet 'normal' people and keep fit.

A man approached the table where I was nursing a cool Club beer. I smiled at him and he drew back a chair.

'Hi, I'm Ralph. Ralph Owens and you?'

''I'm Ewan Shankland. Been here long?' I asked—the usual question.

'Coming up two years,' he said. I knew he was trying to identify me.

'So where do you earn your cedis?' I asked, smiling.

'British High Commission.'

I had to think quickly, take a chance? Now or never—time was running out. My palms were sweating and I felt a panic in my heart. My plan was materialising right before my eyes. 'So where are you on the ladder of progress?' I asked to see where he stood in the ranks.

'Third Secretary. Two off the top but I hope to make

progress as long as I don't blot my copybook,' he laughed and clicked his fingers at a passing waiter. A Guinness was ordered.

'And you? Let me guess. Banker?'

'No, you'd never guess.'

'Okay, then I won't try.'

I took a deep breath.

'I'm a Soviet agent, wanting to defect.'

Ralph laughed loudly—till he saw my sad expression.

A silence grew. His Guinness arrived. He put his lips to the glass and his eyes focused on mine.

'But you are Scottish aren't you?'

I nodded. 'Would it be possible to speak to your ambassador?'

He held his glass in both hands. 'Maybe.' His face turned serious. 'It depends how much you can tell me here and now.'

I asked if he had an hour to spare so my story could be laid bare.

'I've all afternoon, and it looks like overtime for me,' he said rubbing his hands together.

So I told him how I fell into the clutches of the Soviets, and how the chocolate's I delivered in Sandema killed a traitor to their cause and four African children. I also warned him that the Russians knew about how the diplomatic car scheme was being exploited by his own staff. He took considerable interest in that.

'Tell me again, how did you find that out?'

And I told him. He could see the honesty in my eyes as I began to reveal myself. It made him uncomfortable. He shifted from one buttock to the other. I could see he was ill at ease.

'So it's all about choosing the correct timing. I want my fiancée back in the UK before I make my move,' I told him.

'When is she leaving?'

'Next Friday.'

'So you are looking for political asylum?'

'Exactly and I'll spill the beans on the Russians in Ghana and London too,' I said making an offer he could not refuse.

'What time is her flight?'

'It's a midday flight to London, then a hop up to Glasgow.'

'I see. Could you be at the British Embassy by 1:30 pm after she has flown?'

Chapter 24
Asylum denied –
Morag Flies Home

That night I went to see Morag. She told me how much she had enjoyed the last six weeks, and how she was looking forward to getting home to show her parents her engagement ring.

'But how long will it be before you come home?' she asked.

'I've made some progress there,' I began.

'Not flying home from Bolivia then?'

I patted her arm playfully. I shook my head. 'If I play my cards right I'll be home a few days after you.'

'You seem confident.'

'I suppose I am. I have a golden bullet for the British Embassy. I think they'll like what I have to say.'

Morag dropped her head at a rakish angle and raised her eyes in a teasing manner. 'Normality is all I want. A stable life—to have a family one day. Is that too much to expect?'

'Trust me Morag,' I said.

She looked at her watch. 'Do you have to be home tonight?'

'No, they think I'm making myself useful.'

'I'd prefer you were making yourself useful to me.'

She kicked off her shoes, grabbed my T-shirt and we flopped onto the bed.

Morag's departure day arrived and I was there to help her do her final packing. What seemed like a multitude of medical professionals called at her room that morning. I realised if I had not already, that she had been made very welcome, been enthusiastic in her work and become popular with the staff.

The hospital paid for a taxi to the airport. In the back-seat, Morag tapped my bag. 'What have you got in there?'

'Essentials. I'll need them tonight.'

Fear gripped her. 'Darling, do be careful.'

I hoped a reassuring smile would placate her, but we both felt our separation looming and neither of us could be certain when we would meet again. Separation would be even more painful now that we were engaged.

Caledonian Airways efficiently sent her baggage through the lines then we loitered in the departure lounge holding hands. The heat of the day was at its peak outside, but inside, the high fans gave some considerable relief. They resembled the propellers of older aircraft – wafting a steady flow of cool air. I held my anxiety in check, doing my best to hide it from Morag.

'Give me a call as soon as you land in the UK, won't you?' she asked.

'Don't worry, of course, I will—I hope sooner than you expect.'

Small talk and sentiments of mutual love were expressed until Morag's flight was called. It heightened my anxiety further and sweat began to form on my brow, I wiped it off with my handkerchief. No sooner than the handkerchief was out of sight than Morag gave me a hugging clenched kiss. I held her tightly for as long as I could. The second call for the flight was announced and we let go of each other.

I stood and watched her disappear and I was all alone once more. It gave me the impetus to sort out my situation.

I left the airport and hailed a taxi.

'Osu R.E. please, British High Commission.'

Why the R.E had not been dropped, I did not know. The Royal Engineers had long since left. But by the same token, it was another link by which the Commonwealth remembered the days of the Gold Coast.

The British Embassy office was in Jamestown. I climbed the royal blue carpeted stairs and entered to face a highly polished oak reception desk. 'Good afternoon. My name is Robert Harvie. I believe I am expected.'

My heart was beating like a native drum. The Ghanaian secretary took a moment to flip through some messages on her desk.

'One moment, Mr Harvie. Do take a seat.'

I sat down where she pointed. I was not yet securely on British territory but when my head was raised I was looking into the eyes of Her Majesty in a frame. Then fear gripped me. Who might enter as I waited? My eyes fixed on the door and my ears were alert to any sound on the staircase.

After a couple of minutes a side door opened and Ralph Owens appeared.

'Mr Harvie, thank you for arriving so promptly. Let's go to my office.'

I stood up and followed him along a narrow corridor. On the walls were familiar pictures; the Tower of London, Carmarthen Castle, Giant's Causeway on Northern Ireland's coast and a scene from the highlands of Scotland. I turned my head to see The Tower of London again. Could I end up there, I wondered. Was treason still a crime with a hanging sentence? He showed me into his room. His name was boldly outlined on his door.

'I had imagined meeting the ambassador himself,' I said finding the courage to show my expectations.

'You will meet him, but not just yet. Be patient. I'd like to clarify some points. Your fiancée? Has she left?'

'Yes, just over an hour ago.'

He scribbled that information down.

'You indicated at the Labadi club that you had information to tell us.'

I told him about the Russian London staff and the Tamale situation. The IRA's intentions on the mainland and I began to tell him about the British car scam, but he raised his pen to his lips.

'We've sorted that.'

The telephone rang. He picked it up and nodded a couple of times. 'Yes, sir…yes… right away.' Then he put the telephone back on its cradle.

'The Ambassador is ready to see you.'

I was led further down the corridor to a sharp left turn. At the end were two rooms. The smaller one was for the ambassador's secretary and the other was the ambassador's. Ralph knocked then entered, beckoning me to follow. Sir William Copland, the British Ambassador, stood up.

'Mr Harvie, please have a seat.'

Ralph handed Sir William a brown file. As he did so I caught a glimpse of my name on the cover. Then he left.

'This is a very unusual case, as it were. Fortunately, you met Mr Owens at the pool. That gave us some time to check your credentials.'

I swallowed some saliva and waited to hear what else he knew about me.

'You say the Russians know about the car dealings within my office?'

I took a breath. 'Yes. But I informed Mr Owens about it.'

He nodded. 'We've identified two members of staff who ran the illicit business. They have been dismissed from the service. They are no longer in Ghana.'

That statement made me feel relieved. It was a good defence if the Russians made more of the case.

'But let me come to your situation. You seek asylum. Well, if you want to return home to Scotland, that's not asylum. I can't grant that. You are merely going home.'

My heart sank. I needed some sort of protection if I was not to stay in Ghana, or if I was evading being sent to Bolivia. I explained the situation to him more comprehensively.

'There is a way to safeguard your identity. But first, what are your intentions when you get home?'

I gathered my thoughts. 'Wait till my fiancée graduates and get married. By then I'll probably be a teacher.'

'It's not as easy as that, is it?'

I had no answer to his question, and he knew I knew it from the vacant expression on my face.

'You think you can just go home and live in Glasgow and not attract interest from the Soviets? Nor would you have made any preparations to go to Bolivia,' he said drilling his eyes into mine.

I wondered how the interview might end. I did not like the way it was going. The ambassador was well informed about me.

'Mr Harvie, it's not going to be like that, I assure you. First MI5 will have to meet you on your arrival in London. And Mr Harvie, you will no longer exist.'

My eyes screwed up. God, what does he possibly mean?

He opened his drawer and brought out a dark blue passport. He passed it to me over his desk.

'Study it carefully.'

I opened it. It bore the shield of the United Kingdom of Great Britain and Northern Ireland. The number in the white oblong box at the bottom was Lo 627747 but on the familiar dark blue passport was the name, Mr P.E. Clark.

I opened it to read the first page. Mr Peter Ewart Clark, Citizen of the United Kingdom and Colonies. I turned to the next page and saw more familiar entries. 6th October 1950. My date of birth was correct. Height, 5ft 11" correct; colour of eyes, blue – correct; colour of hair, black that was hardly true. Whether bleached by the African sun or not, I had always had fair hair. It seemed the only error. The next page announced the passport was valid for all parts of the Commonwealth and for all Foreign Countries. It was dated by the Liverpool regional passport agency two months ago. On the same page, it had an entry for a profession.

'So, I am Peter Ewart Clark, journalist?'

'Just imagine you are Robert Harvie back home in Glasgow, having broken all communication with their embassies in both London and Accra. How quickly could they find you? Almost instantly, I assure you. What could they do to you? Well you know what they do to defectors— don't you?' he asked with a grin.

My memory focussed for a moment on Lorenzo Desoto and the box of chocolates.

'My advice is never to take sweets from a stranger, not so?' he laughed, then stopped abruptly. Perhaps he was remembering the four dead children.

'I suppose so. I just hope my fiancée sees it the same way.'

'I wouldn't worry too much about that. She has the choice of a dead Robert Harvie or a new life as Mrs Morag Clark, I'm sorry, I mean Dr Morag Clark.'

I found myself nodding at what the ambassador had just said. It looked like I would be making the flight home and a few necessary adjustments to my life had to be made. I could cope but there were some points to clarify.

'If I'm a journalist, who do I write for? That's not clear,' I said.

He smiled knowingly. 'Freelance of course. You write for whoever buys your story.'

That seemed a good cover. If anyone asked I could say I had written for the Times, the Guardian, the Daily Mail, and the Glasgow Herald. Ah, of course, didn't the Telegraph send me out to do an article about Ghana. Who would check? My cover seemed good.

I noticed the ambassador's face grew concerning. 'Unfortunately, the next flight to London is Monday night, arriving in London in the early morning of Tuesday. You will be met by MI5.'

Being back in London sounded great, as long as I kept clear of the Russian embassy. But that raised another problem.

'What if the Soviets find me and want me to do something on Monday? That would cause difficulty,' I suggested, biting my lower lip.

His smile disarmed me.

'You will be staying at the Presbyterian church compound at Kuku Hill. That's about a mile away, but Mr Owen will take you there.'

'Thanks, that will be a great help for me, it truly will be.'

'There will be some conditions. Firstly, you must not leave the compound for any reason. Remember now that Morag has gone; the Soviets will notice your absence more. You no longer have a reason not to be at their embassy overnight. Secondly, your meals will be brought to you. We have left a couple of novels you can read.'

'Thank you. You have been very busy on my behalf. I really do appreciate what you are doing for me.'

'Let's not count our chickens yet, Mr Harvie. You will be driven to the airport on Monday night but unfortunately, a Russian flight will have landed shortly before you take off. We can expect some of your former colleagues to be around at that time.'

'Oh dear, that could prove difficult.'

'Of course, it will. However, we have arranged for that too.'

He lifted his telephone and moments later I was being driven up the hill to Kuku Hill for a weekend in nerve-wracking detention.

Chapter 25
Kuku Hill, Accra

The church and its buildings were in a walled compound. The entrance had a mesh gate and a Muslim night watchman in a flowing gown prepared for his evening prayers while keeping a watchful lookout. I was impressed that the church had prepared a wudu room for cleansing preparations for him.

My room was sparse. It had light green painted walls, a mosquito net over the open window and a single bed. There was no shade on the light. I shared the room with several moths. I flopped down on the solid bed and promptly fell asleep.

It was dark when I woke. I turned on the light, but rather than flying to it, my friendly moths seemed to have flown away. I had the surreal thought that the moths had flown to the Russian embassy and informed my former handlers where I was staying. I grinned at my stupidity. But I was far from being at ease.

I heard a bell ring. It seemed to come from the far end of the building. I went out on to the balcony of what was the Victorian Basle mission house. From the darkness, I heard a woman call out.

'Mr Clark, your supper is ready.'

I came down to the ground floor and made my way to

the dining room. There was one man engaged in his meal, dipping his right hand into the fufu and gathering some palm nut soup. As he did so, he made a slurping noise. I acknowledged him with a nod, which made him point to the chair opposite him. I sat down.

'Are you a new missionary?' he asked.

I hesitated, looking at my approaching meal.

'No, not the church.'

'Funny that. I saw you as a pastor, an agriculturalist, a doctor or a teacher perhaps, a missionary anyway.'

'I must have that common look then,' I said.

'Then you're a spy.'

I looked at his face. He remained fixed on his plate of fufu.

'Good heavens, no. What made you think of that?' I asked with a disarming smile, hiding my anxiety. How could he have known?

'I met a white man here in Accra, a Spaniard. He said his friend was murdered in the north. Talk was that he was a spy, even more so, when he was murdered.'

'Murdered? I didn't hear about that.' I hoped I was convincing.

'You could not have been in Ghana at that time. It was all over the papers.'

'I guess it would be. So this Spaniard, was he a spy or a missionary?' I asked.

'I don't really know what he did. I never asked him.'

On Saturday morning I managed to wash some clothes. I thought they'd dry quickly in the sun, but it was so very humid that day that they took longer than I expected. In the afternoon I heard shouting coming in waves over the compound. I made an enquiry and the maid laughed.

'It's from the El Wak stadium. Oly Dade is playing Accra's Hearts of Oak.'

'Oly Dade?'

'Great Olympics Accra football team. We call them Oly Dade. They are playing Accra Hearts of Oak sporting club.'

'I see. They make a lot of noise.'

'You can hear the game on the radio. Have you got one?'

'A radio? No.'

'Then I bring one to your room.'

And within a few minutes, she was as true as her word. I listened to the end of the first half and got the whole of the second. Oly Dade lost 4-3 in what must have been a very exciting match. Perhaps the goalkeepers were the weak links in each team.

Night fell between 6 p.m. and half-past six. It varied no more than that all year as Accra on the coast is just 4 degrees north of the equator.

As lights flickered on, over the compound wall I heard a car approach. I caught a fleeting glimpse of it as it parked on the far side of the building, but no more.

I heard some footsteps on the wooden staircase to the landing of my room and went out to see who was approaching. It was a Ghanaian with a large box. The man behind him put my mind at rest.

'Mr Clark, a visitor for you.'

'Ah, Mr Owen, I'm afraid I've no hospitality to offer you here.'

'Call me Ralph, we seem to know each other pretty well by now.'

'We certainly do, Ralph. So what's with this box? I won't fit into that,' I said laughing.

'It's not to get into. Let's see what's in it. This is Christian by the way. Can we come in?'

They entered my room and Christian opened the box and laid out some suits, ties, and shoes.

'Here's a suitcase for all your current clothes.'

I opened it and agreed it would take all I managed to bring with me. 'A red tie is out of the question for a start.'

'Good point,' Ralph said rolling up the tie in his hands. 'It's more a matter of what fits. The icing on the cake is still to come.' A wicked smile came over his face.

'Am I getting my passport back yet?' I asked.

'Not just yet, Robert. You will see why in a moment.'

It was plain that he was not ready to tell me everything.

I tried on the shirts with a 14-inch collar. I laid out two ties which seemed to match like cup and saucer. A pair of size eight brown shoes fitted like gloves—I was pleased with my new outfit.

'So where's the icing?'

'Okay take off your shirt and come through to the bathroom.'

Christian had filled the sink with lukewarm water and placed a stool in front of it. In his hand, he had a bottle.

I bent over the sink and closed my eyes. His hands rubbed my scalp as if he were vigorously scratching a dog. It was pleasant—the first time I had had my hair washed by anyone since I was a small boy. When he had finished I opened my eyes to see the water as black as coal. He wiped my face clean and I stood in front of the mirror. My fair hair was as black as the night. He asked me to sit down once more.

'I brought Christian along because he is a barber.'

He cut my hair and gave me a central parting. Now my face in the mirror was unrecognisable – even to me. Goodness knows what Morag would think.

A close-up photo was taken. In fact, three were taken. I realised why.

'You guys are very thorough. I bet you have done this before.'

It was a somewhat rhetorical question and it deserved the lack of a reply it got.

They stayed a further half hour, making sure I had made no other arrangements and that I would be ready at 6 p.m. on Monday evening to be driven to the airport, two hours before departure. I'd get my passport back then. Indeed it would show me with black hair and a somewhat comical central parting. At least that was how I saw it.

On Sunday it was far from quiet. Church bells woke me and the voices of choirs seemed to be everywhere. I found myself kneeling beside my bed. It was a prayer I felt I had to make, to help secure my return home without incident and to give me a sense of calm courage.

I could not eat breakfast. My stomach was in a spin. So I walked around the compound boundary wall like a caged prisoner waiting for his execution.

That afternoon, I slept like a newborn chimp but with no mother's breast to cling to. When I awoke, the afternoon light was beginning to fade. My final preparations to leave Ghana were underway.

It was a black air-conditioned Daimler, Corps Diplomatique, of course. The flag on the bonnet was covered, which indicated that the British Ambassador was not inside.

I sat in the back with Ralph. As the car approached the diplomatic residential quarters I sat back and slunk down in the seat. Meanwhile, my heart was bounding like a cheetah.

Ralph told me we were passing the Russian embassy. I ignored, with a nervous laugh, his invitation to stop and say my fond farewells.

Ralph shook my hand. 'I will stay with you at the airport, but I thought I'd like to shake the hand of a defecting Russian spy. We don't deal with many of them.'

'A very reluctant spy you mean? I was trapped from the day I wrote to them, to correct an error on the radio. It was so easy to get pulled further into their web.'

'Seems so. Anyway, we are about to get you out. Remember to relax. You will be with your fiancée very soon.'

The luxurious car slowed down and the driver came to open my door. The oven-like heat of the country hit me once more.

Inside the airport, there were traders selling fruit, Pioneer biscuits and sweets. Pioneer seemed to a popular product name. I ignored all of them. British Caledonian would provide a sumptuous meal and I had that on my mind momentarily while a more pressing matter took over.

'Am I getting my passport back yet?'

'Yes, sorry. Gosh I should have given it to you in the car.'

Ralph handed the passport to me keeping his hand over its front face as he did so.

'Okay, I'll stand over there.' He pointed to a window from where he could watch the runway. 'You book in your baggage then come back to me.'

The British Airways check-in desk was staffed by a local Ghanaian woman. I stood in line and watched her as she checked through the passengers ahead of me. She did so very efficiently without making much eye contact. Unusually for a Ghanaian, she seemed cold, almost uninterested in her work. There was a minimum of conversation made.

I approached her with my ticket, passport and luggage. I saw her name was Betty. She took my case, labelled it and placed it on a series of metal rollers. She gave the case a kick and it disappeared through a dark plastic sheet taking it out of sight.

Suddenly she smiled at me. 'So, what do you write?'

I was taken aback. 'Oh, lots of things,' I said as my mind went into overdrive.

'What did you cover in Ghana? What have you said about us?'

'Good things. You are a friendly country with beautiful

countryside, wildlife and a great supply of fruit and vegetables,' I smiled.

'But you have not been to the north. It's almost a desert. Did you know that?'

'Indeed I do, I visited Tamale and Bolgatanga,' I thought that would show I had covered her country from head to toe.

'Did you write about the murders in Sandema?' she asked looking up at me.

I realised I had been stupid to mention the north.

'I arrived too late to cover the story. Anyway, the investigation wasn't making any progress. It lacked interest for the papers in Europe,' I said returning my eyes to my passport in her hands.

She snapped the passport shut. 'Have a good flight, Mr Clark.' I thanked her and placed my new passport in my back pocket.

'Next please,' she said even before had I left her desk.

I returned to Ralph.

'So far, so good.'

He took my wrist.

'Don't speak too soon. The Russian plane has just landed. Let's sit over here besides some other travellers.'

We made our way over to a couple of vacant seats and sat down. Ralph had brought a *Daily Graphic*. He handed it to me.

'Now cross your legs and bend over as if it is the most interesting thing you have ever read.'

I looked at the second back page, which featured a report of the Accra Olympics v Hearts of Oak game I had heard on the radio. I became engrossed in the report. As I turned back a page, I looked up. Standing only a few feet from me was Vitaly Karmanov, First Secretary of the Russian embassy.

My foot nudged Ralph's shoe. I pointed behind the paper at the figure in front of me. 'Russian diplomat,' I whispered so quietly he bent forward.

'What?'

'I said, Russian—First Secretary,' and pointed my finger as discreetly as I could.

'Relax Peter,' he replied.

But relax I could not. I turned to another page. Surely all Vitaly could see was a man with black hair and a central parting? For a moment he lingered and then he moved a few paces forward. I glanced up and he shook the hand of a traveller from Moscow. They were all smiles. Vitaly took his luggage and they passed us together. I heard his muffled speech. I wondered if Vitaly was telling him about the Russian speaking Scot who he would meet at the embassy. But it was my imagination out of control. They turned to leave the airport. Vitaly seemed to glance in my direction for a brief moment. Then he made for the exit without any further interest in me.

'The sooner I am onboard the flight the better.'

'We'll just have to wait till it's called, Peter. Relax, you are almost there. Don't go and blow it now.'

Chapter 26
London in Disguise

I looked back on the past hour as the plane gathered speed along the runway. When its front wheels left the ground and the plane nosed skywards, I gasped. When the rear wheels lifted and the roofs of Accra grew smaller by the second, I knew I was safe from Russian clutches—for the time being. I relaxed more than I thought I ever could.

Before too long that longed-for evening meal was served and coffee followed. When the trays were gathered, the lights were dimmed. I placed the dark shades over my eyes, let my seat go back a few inches, took a deep breath and entered the land of Nod.

I awoke around 4 a.m. Most of my fellow passengers were still asleep, but I could not return to that state. I took a page out of a notebook in my bag and began a letter.

We landed at Heathrow at 5:45 a.m. I was not in a rush to leave the security of the plane and continued sitting while other passengers stood impatiently in the passageway. Eventually, they moved off and I brought up the rear.

Would I be briskly arrested by MI5 or would they take a more gentle approach to my detention? Immigration control took a cursory glance at my passport. After all, they could not have been looking for a Russian spy. I was then free to collect my baggage and head for the Customs area. The 'Nothing to Declare' lane formed a queue. It seemed every tenth passenger was asked to show the contents of their cases. I felt we were all counting whether we were the tenth in line. There was no interest in my progress. Then I appeared in the clear, convinced I had an honest face. It did not take long to see three suited men eyeing me. I smiled at them. They smiled back.

'Mr Clark?' the tallest man asked.

'Yes, I was expecting to meet you.'

The car took us to the banks of the Thames. It took more than an hour. Then I was seated behind a table.

'Good morning Mr Clark. I trust you are not too tired after your long flight?'

'No, not at all,' I said apprehensively to a mushroom suited man in his late thirties.

'I am Mr Gray. I need to ask some questions.'

'Of course,' I said wishing to seem obliging.

'I have, of course, received much information about you from Ambassador Copland, in Accra. I'd like to hear your story.'

'I trust you have the time?'

Mr Gray got out his notepad. 'I'm ready when you are, and I've got all day.'

I smiled at the thought because my story was unique. It needed to be told exactly, and above all that required time. For one thing I was certain. I was not a Russian spy.

Two hours later, after one convenience break fuelled by a complimentary coffee, I sat back having told everything I could without any omission.

'Then you will be anxious to see your fiancée,' Mr Gray said with a slight smile.

'You are reading my mind.'

'That's what MI5 does, read minds,' he laughed. His tune changed. 'Of course, this is just your story. I can't risk you still being a Russian spy, returning here to continue to spy for the Soviets.'

Was he teasing me? Why the sudden change of questioning? 'I appreciate some of the information I have given cannot be verified, but I can give you my word. I am no longer anyone's spy.'

'Mr Clark. It's not that I don't believe you. I just cannot take a chance. So where are you heading now?'

'I'd like to phone my fiancée as soon as possible to say I have arrived in London and then get a train north to Glasgow.'

'Very well. I have no objection and no intention of detaining you further. I have just one requirement of you.'

My eyebrows tightened.

'You will report to the nearest police station on the first working day of each month. Do you understand?'

'Yes, but for how long?'

'That is for MI5 to determine, not you, Mr Clark.'

'I see.'

'You wished to make a telephone call? Go next door. It's a small room but has a telephone. Dial 01 to get an outside line.'

I did as I was told and dialled the number which Morag had given me. 'Dr Sutherland?'

'Speaking.'

'It's Robert Harvie here. I've arrived in London. I look forward to seeing soon.'

'Well, you have been a bit of an enigmatic fiancé. We look forward to seeing you again too.'

'Can you get a message to Morag after classes? I assume she is at classes just now.'

'I can phone her flat, later presumably

'Yes, but tell her I love her too,' I added.

'Ah, of course.'

I replaced the telephone and returned to the interrogation room. It was empty. I left the MI5 building and made my way to Euston station. There, I posted the letter I had written on the plane.

Clearly Dr Sutherland had got his message through to Morag. I saw her on the forecourt of Glasgow Central station looking at the passengers leaving the London train. Her gaze passed over me.

I approached her, then stopped and stood still, about ten paces away. She glanced at me briefly and continued her focussed search behind me.

'Is that not Morag Sutherland?' I asked.

Still, there was no recognition but curiosity at what I had said.

'My fiancée, Morag?' I finally blurted out and ran with my arms open. We hugged briefly then we separated.

'Goodness me, you look so different—and to be honest I don't like that central parting.'

'Nor do I, it has got to go.'

'And the black hair?'

'Yes, it's going too. Come on, have you time for a coffee at the station cafe? I've much to tell you.'

Morag could see why the disguise was essential in leaving Accra and offered a restorative procedure back at her flat, dying my hair back to something close to its natural colour. What she had difficulty in accepting was my new name—Peter Clark.

'Darling when we get married does this mean I marry a Harvie or a Clark?'

'Let some water flow under the bridge,' I began, but she stopped me immediately.

'How are you going to explain that you are Mr Clark to my parents?'

I grimaced. 'Well at least you can see why I had to do it.'

'Yes, but my parents have been telling all our relatives and friends that I am engaged to Mr Robert Harvie.'

'I see. So how much do your parents know my background?'

'Not as much as you think. A Post-graduate languages student working with peanuts in Ghana is about as much as I've told them,' she said with a laugh then as we clung together we kissed, like old times.

That night in her flat Morag asked me about the possible charges I might face over the five murders. Her concentration on me was almost overpowering.

'The case died down after a while,' I said with a sigh. 'But on the plane, I wrote a letter to the Ghanaian High Commissioner in London. I told him about the Russians' plot to assassinate the dissident Lorenzo Desoto using a tin of poisonous Quality Street chocolates. I explained that I was the courier who delivered them to him without knowing their significance. I told him everything, including about the children. I thought it important for them to know.' A tear was not far from falling down my cheek. Morag held my arm and stroked it.

'No one ever planned to murder four innocent children, but the blame has to be laid at the Russian Embassy in Accra for arranging the plot, and to the late Mr Utechin for carrying out the plan through me.'

Once more she looked at me with concern. 'Did you sign the letter?'

I shook my head.

We agreed that that weekend, Morag would go home on Friday night with the sole intention of establishing me in the best possible light. She would give a full explanation of what had happened since we met at university, and how I had been trapped into being a Russian spy. She would say that those days were now over and that the British Ambassador in Accra had given me a new identity. The worst pill to swallow was the fact their daughter was soon to become a Clark and not a Harvie.

That same weekend I went home to my parents to explain my situation. They were mystified that my life could have followed such a path. Yet they saw I had survived and had matured through the process.

On Sunday night back in Morag's flat, we assessed the families' responses.

Morag said, 'Let's give our parents marks out of 10. 10 being no problem and 1 being a disaster and pressure to end our engagement.'

'Wow, two extremes. Okay, we shout the numbers out at the same time, after the count of three. Ready?'

'Just a moment,' she said thinking through her parental encounter. I was sure of my response but hoped our results would be favourable. She nodded that she was ready.

'Okay, 1, 2, 3—8.'

'8' We had shouted in unison. We hugged each other.

'So tell me why not 10?'

Morag spent a thoughtful moment looking towards the ceiling. 'I suppose just the embarrassment they feel having to tell their friends that Robert is really Peter,' she giggled. 'And for you?'

'I suppose I didn't write to them enough. That was the main problem but they are pleased that we have got back together.'

Morag went to the kitchen and opened a drawer.

'Hey, what are you doing?' I asked.
'Making something to eat, that's all.'
'Well stop. Get your coat on.'
'Why?'
'Because I've just booked a table at the Ubiquitous Chip.'

Chapter 27
Postscript

By the time we met our parents again, my hair had found its natural parting, but the black hair was going to take longer to lighten and eventually disappear. In fact, our hair was not too dissimilar in colour. My beard had long since been shaved off.

I resumed studies to gain my teaching certificate and began teaching Spanish and Russian to secondary pupils at Shawlands Academy. The following summer Morag qualified as a doctor and worked at the Victoria Infirmary nearby, where my father was still the hospital's chaplain.

I attended the Stewart Street Police Office monthly on the south side of the city for eighteen months. Thereafter a visit was required every two months and after a further six months, my requirement to report was terminated. In some ways, I enjoyed my visits. I got to know several police officers and found them to be polite and charming, despite seeing them arrive with men in handcuffs swearing like the proverbial troopers. Over the years, no retribution from the Russians came my way and I sometimes mentioned becoming Robert Harvie again but Morag was quite adamant we stayed as we were.

'I'm not changing my name again and nor should you. It's safer this way, for both of us.'

By then we were married and our first baby was on the way. That would be another issue—one day we would have to explain to our child why my surname was not the same as my father's. But children adapt to life's strangeness more easily than we do. I knew that one day my past would have to be shared with the next generation, and I hoped that by then Russia might be a more responsible nation. But I had my doubts.

Two years later I decided to write about my experience. Let me share the first page of the first chapter with you.

CHAPTER 1
Jura 1967

Have you ever been to the island of Jura? Not many people have. If you are a whisky connoisseur you possibly toured the island's distillery to taste Isle of Jura single malt. Perhaps you were a climber assaulting the famous Paps of Jura, or a sailor assessing the treacherous cauldron of the Corryvreckan whirlpool from the safety of land. Maybe you needed to imbibe the presence of George Orwell (aka Eric Blair) who completed *Nineteen Eighty-Four* at Barnhill on the north of the island. That's about all you can do on Jura, which is why not many go there. That however may be its attraction.

I was there during the Cold War years and there my spying career took roots. I was on a family holiday in July 1967. In the third week my life changed forever...

The End

Acknowledgements

Special thanks are due to David Watt, formerly of AFNOR (Association Française de Normalisation) the equivalent of the BSI (British Standards Institute) in the UK. A translator, reviser and proof-reader. What a friend he is indeed. To my agent Mathilde Vuillermoz, who keeps faith with me while answering all my demanding questions. And to Jocelyn who leaves me to daydream, walk the dog, garden, shop, and cook. In the process of these chores, I work out my next line.

Finally, I express my thanks to the Russian State for their gifts and without whom this book would not have been written…even although it does not show the Russian Government in a favourable light.

Interview with the Author

What made you write this book?

After writing *A Reluctant Spy*, I thought about my own brief encounter with the Soviets and spying when I was a schoolboy on holiday on Jura. Yes, the first chapter is true, as is the first part of the second. Once that was written, the brakes were off and a story emerged.

Why did you set the story mainly in Ghana?

Tamale airport in the north of Ghana, during the Cuban Crisis in the cold war, granted landing rights to the Russians. It seemed remote but ideal as a base for espionage. Of course, I did live in Ghana between the years 1972-78 and have visited Sandema, Navrongo, and Tamale in the north, as well as many towns in the south. I worked in Tema where I lived at the Presbyterian Church in Kortu Gon (Community 1). Authors often write about what they have experienced.

Why is the book a novella?

A book is not enhanced by writing more than is necessary. Did I know when I started if it would have been a novella? Yes, I knew the limitations of the storyline and so it is a novella. It also keeps the book very active. The chapters are short. It is easy to read a chapter before going to sleep. Novellas are at last having their day too. It seems we have no appetite for the 500 page novels these days.

Do you distrust Russians?

I admire the Russian people. They suffered much during WW2. They are a responsible peace loving people, as they showed during the World Cup of 2018. Their Government, however, bends the truth and has a hostile attitude to many parts of the world today.

What will your next book be?

After writing *A Reluctant Spy* I had a break from writing. I could not think of a storyline. Then quite by accident I realised my great aunt was not the only spy in the family and this book emerged. I have written twenty-three books. Sometimes two books a year. At present, I have started to write Love Amidst the Flanders Trenches. Then perhaps a comedy book? I'm open to that idea. That should be fun.

However, I have also started work as a Jane Austin Literary mentor supporting evolving writers all over the world. A writing career offers many opportunities. I am delighted to be working with children from Saudi Arabia and Qatar so far. Perhaps I will be reading what Ghanaian children have written soon.

Other books by Miller Caldwell

Novels

Operation Oboe
A Scottish widow becomes a Second World War spy in
West Africa
ISBN 0755200090-X New Generation Publishers

The Last Shepherd
An arrogant city banker clashes with the rural ways of the
last shepherd in south-west Scotland.
ISBN 978-07552-0643-4 New Generation Publishers

Restless Waves
A writer-in-residence aboard a cruise ship faces daemons
onboard and onshore.
ISBN 0-7552-0260-0 New Generation Publishers

Miss Martha Douglas
Martha, a nurse and seamstress obtains a royal position
but becomes a suffragist. When released from prison she
serves in the trenches, where she finds true love.
ISBN 978-0-7552-0689-6 New Generation Publishers

The Parrot's Tale
The comic tale of an escaped parrot in the Scottish
countryside sits alongside the tragedy of a missing girl.
ISBN 978-1-910256-05-3 New Generation Publications

Betrayed in the Nith
In this modern romantic novel set in south-west Scotland,
fraternal devotion turns to an unexpected romance as the
mystery of Danny Kimber's death comes to light.
ISBN 978-07552-0625-4 New Generation Publishing

The Crazy Psychologist
Set on Rousay in The Orkney Islands, the childhood
difficulties of Dr Angle Lawrence come to light, explaining her
bizarre treatment programmes, while her fragmented family
come to terms with their past, placing her marriage in jeopardy.
ISBN 978-1-910667-24-8 Matador Publishers

The Trials of Sally Dunning and A Clerical Murder
Two novellas in one book
Sally Dunning is autistic. Bullied, defrauded and drugged,
she is not likely to be the best witness as she sees goodness in
everyone. However, a chance meeting on holiday when her
home is burgled turns Sally's life around in a spectacular way.
ISBN 978 1788038 126 Matador Publishers

A Lingering Crime
Jack Watson is arrested and charged with murder. Extradition
takes him to Florida but he has never been there before.
Florida still has the death penalty and his thoughts turn to
the electric chair. But did he know the victim? How could he
be linked to the deceased? As Jack's story emerges we learn of
his troubled past and his need to right wrongs.
ISBN 978 1789014 150 Matador Publishers

A Reluctant Spy
The life story of Hilda Campbell, who became Frau Hilda
Büttner Richter before Lady Hilda Simpson. A double
agent in World War 2. Published by Clink Street.

Biographies

Untied Laces
The author's autobiography
He confronted Osama bin Laden in Abbottabad, brought
an African dictator to tears, and has two international
sporting caps. So why did untied laces trip him up?
ISBN 978-07552-0459-5 New Generation Publications.

Jim's Retiring Collection
The illustrated cartoons and musings of a city and then
rural Church of Scotland minister. Gathered and set in a
biblical context.
ISBN ASIN B00ND 3F7PM New Generation publications

Poet's Progeny
A line of descent of the national bard, Robert Burns
maintains his influence over succeeding generations.
ISBN 0-7552-0178-7 New Generation Publishing

7 point 7 on the Richter Scale
The diary of the camp manager in the NWFP of
the Islamic Republic of Pakistan following the 2005
earthquake. (Profits have gone to Muslim Hands for
earthquake relief)
ISBN 978-0955-47370-8 Alba Publishers

Take the Lead
The quirks of dogs, as experienced by the author over his life in Scotland, Pakistan and Ghana, together with canine poetry with a record of medical advances made by our canine friends understanding human conditions.
ISBN 9-781910256213 Netherholm Publications

Children's books

Chaz the Friendly Crocodile
Chaz the Nigerian crocodile visits a Scottish river to help people keep their towns tidy. Set as a poem, this is a book parents can use to teach their growing children the value of good manners.
ISBN 978-1-84963770-1 Austin Macauley

Lawrence the Lion Seeks Work
There are no more animals in the circus. So what happened when Lawrence the lion went in search of a new job?
ISBN 978-0-75521656-7 Netherholm Publications

Danny the Spotless Dalmatian
Dalmatian puppies have no spots at birth; they appear after three weeks. But Danny's spots never appeared. Follow him as he searches for spots to make him a real Dalmatian.
ISBN 978-1-91066715-6
e-pub ISBN 978-1-910667-16-3
mobi ISBN 978-1-910667-17-0

Self-Help

Have You Seen My Ummm… Memory?
An invaluable booklet for all whose memories are
declining. Student memory tips as well as advice for those
more senior moments to get through life.
ISBN 0-7552-0146-9 New Generation
ISBN American edition 978-1-4327-3364-3 Outskirts
Press

Ponderings IN LARGE PRINT

Poems and short stories, as it says, in large print.
ISBN 0-7552-0169-8 New Generation Publishing.

It's Me, Honest It Is
Commissioned by the NHS nursing service, this is an end-
of-life handbook for individuals to complete.

Coming in 2020

Love in Flanders Trenches
A World War 1 saga of a nurse imprisoned as a suffragist
and released to serve in the trenches, where she eventually
finds love.

Murder at Blackwaterfoot
When a body is discovered on the island of Arran, the
community are impatient to have the case resolved but
when another body is found on the beach, the pressure is
on Constable Rory Murdoch to find the killer.

The truth of this book dies after chapter 1. Now at the end, some more remarkable truth about my life, not as a spy but in a very unusual encounter.

Your extra story

The day I confronted Usama bin Laden

Our border collie, Tâche, died in the first few days of October 2005. I mention this for two reasons. Firstly that it made me feel low and I was not taking in the news every day. Secondly, I was no longer under a canine regime of regular walks. However, at the end of the year, I was reminded about the dreadful earthquake in South Asia on 8th October 2005 by a friendly part-time special police officer who ran a successful Indian restaurant in town. Farooq Ahmed lost his niece in this disaster which killed 75,000, injured as many again and left thousands widowed, orphaned and abandoned. He told me he was going out to the capital Islamabad to manage aid which was arriving in deluge proportions. He knew I had been placing children on supervision or having them fostered in my professional work for Dumfries and Galloway and also knew I had retired recently. He asked if I would be willing to go to the North West Frontier Province of the Islamic Republic of Pakistan to assist in the care of the children in a large camp at Mundihar. With no dog and an un-protesting wife who was prepared for me to go, I set off.

I arrived in Islamabad on 7th January 2006 with a case full of balloons, colouring-in books, exercise jotters, string, and my mouthorgan which security staff both at Heathrow and Islamabad insisted I played to the amusement of other travellers. That was a relief. It showed up on their radar as a gun-sized metal object. They applauded in London as did the staff in Islamabad.

I was driven 130 kilometres into the NWFP to reach the Camp at Mundihar. The ground had been donated by a farmer and lay in snow-covered tiered circles around a gentle hill. 24,500 people lived in tents on this farmland which lacked hygiene, sufficient food and warmth. On the second day, I was called to a meeting outside the farmhouse in temperatures below zero. The atmosphere was tense. A Brigadier of the Pakistani army chaired the meeting. The farmer's wife had been found donating aid to the townsfolk who had not been affected by the disaster. It was a serious matter and the Brigadier made no bones about the situation. I raised my hand. The Brigadier looked up and gave me his attention. I spoke of world disasters and how people instinctively donated food, clothing and money to aid charities. Such aid came flying out to where it was needed but there was often no administration on hand to deliver it. I saw this as a similar situation. What was needed was a responsible structure and rotas so everyone receives aid and knows when it is arriving.

The brigadier stood up and pointed at me. 'Sir, you are not a Muslim.' I acknowledged his statement with a nod. 'You are independent. I make you the camp manager.' Suddenly and unexpectedly I found myself with a job, one which required my attention 24/7 and so my role changed dramatically. It became a job to prioritise the distribution of food and blankets – a priority in the cold and frosty January weeks. There were feuds to resolve amid pointed Kalashnikovs but I kept mine safe in the tent I slept in, as it was suggested to me by the Brigadier who provided it for me. Rain seeping down the terraces caused fury again when arms were the way the residents resolved disputes. Then I took ill.

I lost all energy and came down with influenza-like symptoms. I was taken to a building to recover in Mansehra where underneath a banner, Muslim Hands Eye Clinic, I lay on a mattress semi-conscious. After two days I was beginning to feel better and sat up on my floor bedding. Then I heard a car enter the compound. Two car doors closed, one after the other.

There did not seem to be anyone else around, so I got up and went to the door. On the compound ground before me stood a very tall man. The tallest man I had seen in Pakistan by far. He was about my height, as I stood on the raised forecourt step. He wore a cream chemise. His face was long with a straggly grey beard and piercing eyes. He looked very familiar. 'Salaam Alaikum' (Peace be unto you) I said bringing my beard close to his bearded cheek. 'Alaikum Salaam' (And unto you, Peace) he replied. That was when I suspected the most feared man in the world was standing before me. There was a stand-off silence for a moment before he asked of someone of whom I had no knowledge. I told him so.

'Then who are you?' he asked with contorted brows. There was a hint of accusation in his voice as if perhaps he thought I was trying to identify him.

'I am the camp manager at Mundihar. I am recovering here from flu.'

His eyes narrowed as he asked his final question. 'Where are you from?'

I told him 'Scotland' and on hearing this, without any further conversation, he turned and moved as quickly as his lame left leg could travel back to the car with the driver's engine still running. It was a light blue four seated car. He sat in the back, bent double. His associate sat with the driver in the front. The car left the compound at speed and left me dazed as I saw it turn right. I saw the road sign above the compound indicate the direction he was taking – it was the road to Abbottabad. Yes, there was no doubt whatsoever in my mind. Not only by his sudden departure but his stature and perfect English, I had met Osama bin Laden. I returned to my mattress and saw my Kalashnikov. A thought ran through my head of having used it but the consequences I'd face would have been dire.

There was much respect shown to Usama bin Laden locally as one who had stood up to the might of the USA. Furthermore, when I received some visitors that night I was told he was often seen around the shops in Mansehra and Mundihar, towns with a joint population of 4 million people. The date was Sunday 26th February 2006 and Usama had just acquired his home in Abbottabad.

On my return to Scotland, I informed my member of parliament and the Chief Constable about the world's leading terrorist in Abbottabad but they thought I was wrong. Both told me he was hiding in an Afghan mountain retreat. I suspect they thought I was deluded.

On 2nd May 2011 Usama bin Laden paid the price. He was shot by US Seals, in Abbottabad, and buried at sea under strict Islamic laws.

Occasionally I wonder what might have happened had I taken my Kalashnikov with me to the door? Might I have, almost by accident, arrested the world's most wanted man? Or shot him, perhaps fatally? And in the end would whatever might have happened, have made any difference? Osama bin Laden is dead now, but at that moment when we met, he was just another man, like me. In my heart I can not begrudge him those extra five years—clearly, he lived in constant fear of capture or worse, and some might say that was punishment in itself.

Miller Caldwell

Milton Keynes UK
Ingram Content Group UK Ltd.
UKHW012254070324
439090UK00005B/114

9 781913 136789